HERDS OF THUNDER, MANES OF GOLD

HERDS OF THUNDER, MANES OF GOLD

A COLLECTION OF

Horse Stories and Poems

COMPILED AND EDITED BY

BRUCE COVILLE

ILLUSTRATED BY TED LEWIN

Doubleday

NEW YORK LONDON TORONTO SYDNEY AUCKLAND

Published by Doubleday,
a division of
Bantam Doubleday Dell Publishing Group, Inc.,
666 Fifth Avenue, New York, New York 10103

Doubleday and the portrayal of an anchor with a dolphin are trademarks
of Doubleday, a division of Bantam Doubleday Dell Publishing Group, Inc.

Library of Congress Cataloging-in-Publication Data
Herds of thunder, manes of gold: a collection of horse stories and poems/
compiled and edited by Bruce Coville; illustrated by Ted Lewin. —1st ed.
    p.   cm.
Summary: A collection of seventeen stories, poems, and excerpts from books
about horses, by well-known authors over several centuries.
ISBN 0-385-24642-0
    1. Horses—Juvenile fiction.   2. Horses—Juvenile poetry.
3. Children's stories.   4. Children's poetry.   [1. Horses—Fiction.
2. Horses—Poetry.   3. Short stories.   4. Poetry—Collections.]
I. Coville, Bruce.   II. Lewin, Ted, ill.
PZ10.3.H46   1989
[Fic]—dc19   88-34651
                                                                          CIP
                                                                           AC

Designed by Diane Stevenson / SNAP•HAUS GRAPHICS

Copyright © 1989 by Bruce Coville
Illustrations Copyright © 1989 by Doubleday, a division of
Bantam Doubleday Dell Publishing Group, Inc.
All Rights Reserved
Printed in the United States of America

September 1989
First Edition

$\mathcal{A}$cknowledgments

for
Ruth Bennett

$\mathcal{C}$ONTENTS

HERDS OF THUNDER, MANES OF GOLD

$\mathcal{I}$ntroduction

I first met Wee Bit O'Blarney at a horse sale nearly thirty years ago. She was a Welsh Connemara pony, a particularly large breed about half again as tall as the Shetland. She was black with splashes of white, and she had a bit of a temper. I was ten, and I desired her profoundly.

A few days later I was splashing about in a swamp near our house, despite having been given strict orders to keep my clothing dry, when my mother called me to come inside. The state of my clothing was not something to be amused about, and the fact that I had *tried* to stay dry didn't seem to make much difference to my angry father. He was not sympathetic to the fact that wet clothes are just one of those things that happen when kids and swamps get together.

I was punished for disobeying and, with dry clothes and wet eyes, was bundled into the car along with my younger brother. We were heading for my grandparents' farm, which was just around the corner. When we got out of the car, I was astonished to see my grandfather come walking around the corner of the barn, leading Wee Bit O'Blarney.

She was saddled, she was ours, and we were going to be allowed to ride her. Incredible! Tears were turned to joy and joy to mirth when, to my great amusement, the pony ran off with my younger brother. I thought this showed good sense on her part, since he was an enormous pest at the time, although now I can see that he was really no more so than any younger brother. Still, it was fun watching him cling to the saddle, crying out in alarm as Wee Bit went bounding across the pasture.

In the long run, though, Rob had his revenge for my

amusement. For when we added a small Shetland pony named Judy to the barn, Rob and I would ride together—Rob on Judy, myself on Wee Bit. Judy was always quite content to leap the small ditch that crossed the pasture, but Wee Bit would usually balk, and more than once I went flying over her neck to land upon my head.

Despite our misadventures, we would not have traded those ponies for anything. Wee Bit and Judy were a part of our lives then, and we were greatly envied among our friends.

As I began to gather stories for this collection, I looked for horses that you might like to make a part of your life. Searching the past, I found wonderful horses from myth, legend, and fairy tale: winged Pegasus, who carried Bellerophon to battle against the fire-breathing chimera; mighty Bucephalus, beloved of Alexander the Great; and enormous Dapplegrim—quite likely the largest horse ever to appear in a story.

The connection between horses and humans is worldwide and centuries old. So here you will find a thrilling adventure about a young girl on the steppes of Scythia, where ancient tribes banded together to ride against the advances of King Darius of Persia. Marguerite Henry, perhaps the world's most beloved writer of horse stories, takes us to eighteenth-century Morocco to witness the birth of "the King of the Wind." And Marian Bray retells the story of a thrilling race that took place in the early days of California.

Horses are still part of our lives today, of course, and so we have modern stories for you, too—stories such as Nancy Springer's rollicking tale of "Barn Gravity" and Mary Stanton's touching narrative of healing brought about by the gentle magic of "Sunrise."

Despite the range of times and places covered in this book, you will find that there is a common thread running through each of these stories: the love that can bind a human and a

Introduction

horse together. As Rob McLaughlin in "My Friend Flicka" wisely tells his son, Ken, "It is a great thing to be friends with a horse."

Which is exactly what we hope you will find in this collection—horses who will become your lifelong friends.

From such famous steeds as Flicka and Black Beauty to newcomers introduced here for the first time, may these horses live in your imagination and carry you through the fields and forests of your mind for as long as you care to dream of saddles and bridles, four strong legs to gallop, and the wind that whips your face as you ride to adventure.

—Bruce Coville

My Horse

I will not change my horse with any that treads.
He bounds from the earth;
When I bestride him, I soar, I am a hawk.
He trots the air; the earth sings when he touches it.
The basest horn of his hoof is more musical than the pipe
   of Hermes.
He's of the color of the nutmeg and of the heat of the
   ginger.
He is pure air and fire, and the dull elements
Of earth and water never appear in him,
But only in patient stillness while his rider mounts
   him . . .
His neigh is like the bidding of a monarch,
And his countenance enforces homage.

              —William Shakespeare
          (from *King Henry V*, Act 3, Scene 7)

Marian Flandrick Bray lives with her husband in California, where she works in a library and raises guinea pigs. When Marian was in college she used to "green break" colts; that is, she was the first to ride them—and often the first to be thrown by them. Though she has given up that activity, she still rides as often as possible.

In the story that follows Marian combines research and imagination to tell of a race that took place in California over a hundred years ago. While her main character is fictional, the race itself actually occurred.

$\mathcal{F}$ LIGHT

OF THE

$\mathcal{S}$ WAN

Marian Flandrick Bray

"Antonio!"

His mother stood on the back porch, her long skirts swirling around her ankles. Antonio thought she looked like one of the angels etched in the stained windows at church. But unlike he'd respond to an angel, he ignored her and finished buckling a freshly clean bridle.

She called his name again and he thought of running away. But something in her voice spoke of a certain oakwood branch leaning in the corner of the kitchen. So he wrapped the bridle and reins around his waist and ran across the barnyard, hopping around the biddies and their chicks.

He halted before her. "Firewood gone?" he asked, pawing at the ground like a stud colt.

"No, *mi hijo*," she said and handed him a piece of paper with words scrawled on it. "Put this in your pocket. Papa forgot the list. You run down to the store and give it to him."

Antonio folded it carefully and shoved it in his back pocket. From the barn a horse whinnied, and as Mama turned, he grabbed her skirts.

"If I take the mare, I will get there faster, no?"

"You and that horse. At least put your boots on." She smiled gently, but it was lost as Antonio fled into the house, grabbed his soft, calf leather boots, and yanked them on.

Spring had a gentle hand in the Sacramento Valley, and the barn was as cool as a mountain dawn. Bottom, the old gelding, thrust his bony head over the stall door and whickered to Antonio. The boy ignored him and trotted to the end of the barn. A mare, black as a night without stars, snorted and struck the stall door with a narrow hoof. When he held out his hand, empty, she drew back, disappointed.

"Sorry. No tortilla this time." He slipped into the stall and she turned her haunches toward him. "No you don't, you silly, beautiful mare." He put his hand on her hip, trusting her. She switched her tail—hard—then didn't move. He walked to her head.

"Black Swan," he murmured. Her ears fluttered like young birds, as she listened to him whisper to her in kind Spanish words.

She was Australian-bred. From a land of sand and heat. She was a Thoroughbred, the first in California. Most men thought she was worthless, a skinny beast, not fit for much, but Papa liked her enough to purchase her. And Antonio, well, he loved her.

He wasn't sure why exactly, because Papa had bought

other horses equally as beautiful. Perhaps it had to do with her seeming so lost after her long boat trip to California, and the way she would press her nose against his arm as if he reminded her of someone in her home barn, thousands of miles away.

She was a race horse. But she had lost her races—including a race for five thousand pesos last year. Antonio bit his lip. That was a lot of money.

Antonio bridled Black Swan with the freshly cleaned headstall and led her out into the slanted light. He sprang up on her back. Wriggling close to her curved neck, he nudged her side with his heels, carefully, and they slipped out onto the road like a smooth-running river.

At the store, Antonio carefully tied the mare to a post, being sure to leave her enough rope to stretch, but not enough to tangle up in. He burst through the store door. Several men looked up from sitting around a wooden barrel. Antonio ran up to Papa and handed him the list. "You forgot," he said. Papa drew him to his side.

"Have you seven-league boots to arrive so quickly?" asked Papa.

Antonio smiled. "Sí. Only this one has four-league boots."

Papa and the men chuckled.

"The mare is fast," said Papa firmly, as if he'd been saying it for some time. The men listened politely because his papa was Don Andreas Sepulveda. They always listened to him. The heavy, sweet scent of candy twisted with the salty, broken crackers crumbled in the barrels, and Antonio wished he had some licorice to suck on. He would save some for Black Swan, too; she had a fondness for sugar.

"In fact," Papa was saying, "my mare can outrun your Sarco." Even Antonio was surprised at that. Everyone stared at Governor Don Pio Pico, Sarco's owner.

8

"Your mare, she lost to Ito last year, no? And he was a gelding. Sarco is a stallion. Very hot-blooded."

Papa tightened. "Only a bad day. The mare is young. She looks better all the time."

"If she's so fast," piped up a thin, wiry man, his hand in the cracker barrel, "how can she have such a long body and narrow bones? It's the horse with many big muscles that runs best." Antonio almost believed him, because he was a trainer of fine horses—horses that could jump over six feet, horses that could herd cattle without the help of people.

Papa smiled. "And can you do a good day's work, my slender friend?"

Lots of laughter at that. Then Papa said, "Black Swan has as many muscles as a racehorse. Only hers are stretched out like a dancer's. You don't see them until she uses them."

The men snickered, and one said, "Who wants a dancer? I want a fast horse."

Don Pico smoothed back his sleek hair. Antonio liked Don Pico. He often ate supper at their house, and had taught Antonio how to tie trick knots and make coins vanish into thin air.

"My mare against your stallion," said Papa. "Five thousand pesos."

The storekeeper slammed down his broom and shouted, "A thousand of your finest cattle, Andreas. Everyone knows about your fine cattle, but horses? Hmmm, we shall see."

Papa and Don Pico gazed at each other, Antonio between them, staring at one, then at the other. They were like dogs about to fight. He marveled. He almost expected them to growl.

"One thousand cattle and five thousand pesos," said Papa.

Don Pico nodded and the men shook hands.

"Name the course," said Papa.

"Up a ladder," said the storekeeper. The men laughed,

and the thin, wiry one pretended to throw the storekeeper out the door. Antonio laughed with them as they tussled a moment, then abruptly broke apart, sweating like yearlings at play.

When the men settled down, Antonio watched Don Pico's face as he considered the course. Antonio knew his father's friend had bred his stallion for distance; Sarco could run all day. His pure Spanish blood pulsed in him, wild and strong. Antonio had often petted the golden stallion and watched him fling his silky, scarlet mane.

"The course," said Don Pico. Antonio held his breath. "From the main road by the lake, back to your house." His black hair shone like a crow's wing, almost blue, in the soft gas light.

"Nine miles," said Papa. Antonio sat quiet, running through the path in his mind, remembering certain hollows, large rocks, and the parched dryness of the land there. Perhaps Black Swan would think she was home, in Australia, galloping in the hot sand.

"When?" asked Papa.

"Four Sundays from the last," said Don Pico. A horse whinnied outside. "After Mass."

"Four Sundays then," said Papa. The men around the barrel murmured in agreement. "And five thousand pesos to the winner, plus one thousand head of fine-blooded heifers."

"Cattle," insisted Don Pico. "I don't want to wipe you out."

Papa put his head close to his friend's and said in a hard voice, "My Thoroughbred will win." He drew Antonio even closer so the boy smelled Papa's warm scent. "This will be my rider."

Antonio felt himself shiver with joy and fear as Don Pico nodded. "Less weight than her last race. Over a mile it might help, but nine miles? Not likely."

Papa shrugged. "Black Swan would run riderless and win or with much weight on her back and still win."

They had a month to prepare.

At first Papa rode the mare, exercising her, with Antonio following on faithful Bottom. The old gelding groaned and grunted, trying to keep up, but Black Swan always flew far ahead.

"But not fast enough," said Papa as they pulled up one bright morning. Bottom's graying muzzle touched the mare's flank, and she whirled, teeth snapping, eyes livid. The gelding hastily backed up. Antonio smiled at her fury because she was so beautiful, so proud.

Papa steadied the mare and said, "You ride Black Swan often, no?"

He looked up, his image mirrored in Papa's eyes. "Sí, Papa," and dropped his head in fear of having done something wrong.

"How does she gallop for you?"

A bird exploded out of a manzanita bush. Bottom merely wiggled his chin whiskers, but Black Swan gave a gulping whinny and reared straight back. Papa reined her down and she struck the ground heavily. Antonio would have been different with her. He would have touched her neck with kind fingers, asking her to return to the ground like a normal beast and not a bird because time for flying would come later.

He considered Papa's question, his fingers mixed with Bottom's thin mane and the reins. "She goes like"—he paused and fussed with the reins, untwisting them—"like her name. A swan in flight."

"And you have seen a swan flying, let alone a black swan?"

Antonio's heart jumped like a caught foal. His father was so serious. "No, Papa, but I can imagine. She moved very well for me."

"Better than she did against Ito?"

Black Swan pawed the hard ground, hearing her name. Her black tail snapped over her hocks.

"*Sí*, better than she did against Ito."

Papa persisted. "Better than she does with me?"

Antonio stared hard at his fingers clutching the braided reins. Each length of leather had been carefully woven. He knew, because he had watched Papa patiently braid them. "*Sí*, Papa," he said softly.

Papa touched his heels to Black Swan. She sprang off her hocks and cantered down the path, Bottom galloping behind. "Good," said Papa. "You will exercise her from now on. No need to round up the heifers."

Antonio sat on Bottom's back, his mouth a circle.

Race Sunday rose like a fledgling, quick and gentle. But by the time Mass was over the sky had hardened into a deep blue.

Papa, astride Bottom, led Black Swan to the lake. Antonio walked behind them, his ebony eyes liquid and large as the mare's eyes, except where his were gentle, worried, hers were stretched, the whites showing. She knew. She was bred to know instinctively when a race was to occur. So she pranced and jiggled and Antonio smiled, watching Papa trying to contain her.

He heard a sound behind them and turned to see the governor on his stallion.

"Here comes Don Pico," called Antonio. Black Swan turned at his voice, and at the sight of the stallion she wrought the air with neighs.

Sarco remained silent, but his eyes bulged. Don Pico grinned at Antonio and caught up with Papa. The men talked and laughed while Antonio studied the stallion. He was a brilliant dun, with gold flecks parading over his coat. His muscles bunched under him as if he were about to leap at any moment. Antonio turned and looked at Black Swan again. She was so different from Sarco—a head taller, leaner, more streamlined. Even her crinkly black tail was longer. Antonio chuckled as she turned her narrow face to snap at the stallion.

When they reached the small lake, Antonio was surprised to see so many people. Horses and riders darkened the shore and muddied the water. A few days before, Papa had showed Antonio newspaper articles which told of the race. As far south as Los Angeles, people were betting great amounts, even whole ranches, on Sarco and the foreign mare, but mostly on Sarco.

The thought seeped into Antonio that most of the men were sympathetic, but most thought Black Swan would lose. Again. His mouth tightened with anger. She would not lose. Not if he could help it.

His anger vanished like a startled bird as Papa lifted him by the seat of his pants onto the mare. She turned her head and nuzzled his boot. The men would be surprised when she won.

The mare lifted her head, her scythe-shaped ears flickering. Hadn't he crouched over her neck when they overtook fleet mule deer in the hills? Hadn't they galloped faster than Papa's hunting dogs as they pursued rabbits? Surprised. The men would be surprised.

Papa put his square hand on Antonio's thigh. "The path is narrow, so try to get in front immediately. Then slow her down to conserve her strength. If Don Pico moves off the path to pass, you stay parallel with him. If he does get ahead, you stay on his heels. Remember this is a nine-mile race, Antonio. Don't push her beyond what she can do. We know she is the fastest, but you must be the smartest."

13

Antonio nodded. His hands were clammy on the reins. But the wind would whip them dry once the mare ran. His stomach trembled like a mare's before she foals.

The storekeeper, long stick in his hand, drew a deep line in the dirt. Dust ruffled up in the still, hot air. "Line up!" he shouted. Papa released the reins and Antonio gathered them in his shaking hands. He watched Papa walk away, then turned the mare to face the starting line.

Sarco strode up. His coat gleamed golden brown like Mama's tortillas. Don Pico sat astride him, deep in his silver-trimmed saddle. Sarco nickered very low to the mare. Her ears flashed back and she bared her teeth at them.

"No saddle, little one?" asked Don Pico.

Antonio shook his head and twisted his fingers deep in Black Swan's mane. A saddle didn't allow one to feel the horse. Antonio wanted to feel her every move. She pulled at the curb bit, but his hands spoke to her: *Not yet. Only wait but a moment.*

"Ready?" asked the storekeeper. Antonio and Don Pico nodded. "Remember," he added, "the race starts when the gun goes off. I know you'll both be fair and stay true to the course." He aimed his pistol skyward. "On your mark, get set—" The words drew out like a piece of elastic.

Antonio tightened his legs. Black Swan came up against the bit, quivering. He stared out over the empty path.

"Go!" The gun went off and the stallion and mare leaped. Sarco sang into the lead, his golden tail flipping in Black Swan's face.

The path narrowed as it crested the hill.

Riding hard on Sarco's heels, Antonio wondered briefly if Papa were worried. Perhaps he prayed. Who was the patron saint of horses? He should have asked before this race. Then he firmly guided his thoughts to the race.

The path was familiar to him and the mare. She often

grazed along it with Papa's cattle. And she frequently carried Antonio to many of his secret hideouts.

The mare breathed lightly, but he felt the warm prickliness of her sweat through his pants. Two more hills were tackled and overcome. Still no place to pass Sarco safely. They would have to wait for a draw. Until then he guided the big mare on Sarco's tail, choking on the stallion's dust.

The sun was fierce, unyielding. The mare was sweating more, little rivulets trickling down her neck and shoulder. Antonio was getting tired of seeing the stallion's golden haunches and having rocks strike his face. They would pass. Soon.

A small wash tumbled down from a hill, crossing their path and running alongside them. This was where he could pass.

"Gallop," he said. Black Swan flicked her ears back and lengthened her stride. Antonio remembered what Don Pico had said last night when the grown-ups thought he was asleep. He'd listened, crouched beside his bedroom door. The man had said, "The mare is attractive. Clean legs. She and Sarco could produce a fine colt." Antonio had heard his Papa grunt in agreement. But the boy had been furious. Black Swan didn't need a colt to prove herself. She was enough.

He leaned over her shoulders and guided her off the path and into the wash. The sand was deep and she had to lift her hooves high, but she still flew past the stallion who snorted and the man whose eyes opened wider.

Antonio and the mare drew ahead and onto the path. The mare's long tail snapped in Sarco's face.

As Papa had said, Antonio slowed Black Swan down. The mare fought the bit a moment, then yielded. "To save your strength, little bird," he said and felt his heart fill because he was in charge of her. He would help her win.

Each time Don Pico attempted to guide Sarco off the path, Antonio dug his heels into Black Swan's ribs and she kicked

16

ahead. Antonio heard Don Pico swearing and he laughed at each word. It was like a seesaw. The stallion would begin to surge, and Black Swan would meet the challenge and the stallion would fall back.

The miles thundered away.

As they crested the knoll near home, Antonio knew everyone could see them now. The crowd milled around his home. The chickens would be upset, he thought. All the noise and confusion.

Black Swan didn't care about the chickens or the crowds, so she stretched herself out, her quick gaze keeping her from tripping. Sarco roared beside them, Don Pico leaning over his neck and shouting abuse. The whip rose and fell beside them. The golden body gleamed as shoulders, ribs, flanks, and tail feathered by.

Antonio spoke quietly to Black Swan, "Gallop."

And she did.

Her narrow face pushed out and her wide nostrils flared red. She reached mightily and he strained with her. The barn flew by. He heard the chickens squawking, upset as he thought they'd be, and wondered if Mama was on the porch, watching.

He saw the finish line and Sarco ahead.

Quickly he brought the ends of the reins against Black Swan's shoulders—hard. She leaped, almost out from under him, her breath screaming. The golden hide of Sarco went by again, only in reverse: tail, flanks, ribs, shoulders. Black Swan smoothed faster and Antonio struck her once more, to be sure they didn't see the stallion again.

They didn't.

The finish line, deeply drawn in the dirt, exploded under the mare's hooves.

He allowed her to gallop down the road a bit and then pulled her up. She protested once, yanked at the bit, but realized the race was over. He sat stiff, upright, wondering what next, her sweat soaking his legs.

Don Andreas Sepulveda appeared beside them on Bottom, and Antonio slid off Black Swan into his father's arms. Black Swan tossed her head, the reins flying, and minced over to the side of the road. She began to graze. Nineteen minutes and twenty seconds of racing left her hungry. Antonio smiled at the sound of her teeth clicking.

"Black Swan," Antonio found his voice, "Black Swan, look what I brought you." Still on Bottom and in Papa's arms, he drew out a tortilla, round and fresh, and held it out. The mare lifted her head, ignored them, and flattened her ears as Sarco and Don Pico rode past. Then she walked over and neatly took the tortilla. She ate it and shook her head, showering foam over Antonio and Papa, who smiled and smiled into her skinny, Thoroughbred face.

No author is more closely identified with horse stories than Marguerite Henry—and with good reason. Her wonderful books include Misty of Chincoteague, Brighty of the Grand Canyon, *and* Justin Morgan Had a Horse. *Part of what makes a Marguerite Henry story so special is her meticulous research, which helps her bring far-off places to vivid life—as you will see in these pages from* King of the Wind. *The book, which tells the story of the Godolphin Arabian, was awarded the Newbery Medal in 1949.*

THE
BIRTH OF A KING

Marguerite Henry

(from *King of the Wind*)

In the northwestern slice of Africa known as Morocco, a horseboy stood, with broom in hand, in the vast courtyard of the royal stables of the Sultan. He was waiting for dusk to fall.

All day long he had eaten nothing. He had not even tasted the jujubes tucked in his turban nor the enormous purple grapes that spilled over the palace wall into the stable yard. He had tried not to sniff the rich, warm fragrance of ripening pomegranates. For this was the sacred month of Ramadan when, day after day, all faithful Mohammedans neither eat nor drink from the dawn before sunrise until the moment after sunset.

The boy Agba had not minded the fast for himself. It was part of his religion. But when Signor Achmet, Chief of the Grooms, commanded that the horses, too, observe the fast, Agba's dark eyes smouldered with anger.

"It is the order of the Sultan!" the Signor had announced to the horseboys. And he had cuffed Agba on the head when the boy showed his disapproval.

Of the twelve thousand horses in the Sultan's stables, Agba had charge of ten. He fed and watered them and polished their coats and cleaned their stalls. Best of all, he wheeled the whole string into the courtyard at one time for their exercise.

There was one of the ten horses to whom Agba had lost his heart. She was a bay mare, as fleet as a gazelle, with eyes that studied him in whatever he did. The other nine horses he would lead out to the common water trough to drink. But for his bright bay he would fill a water cask from a pure spring beyond the palace gates. Then he would hold it while the mare sucked the water, her eyelashes brushing his fingers as she drank. For long moments after she had drunk her fill, she would gaze at him while the cool water dribbled from her muzzle onto his hands.

It was the mare that worried Agba now as he worked to fill in the time until the hour of sunset. The courtyard was already swept clean, but Agba pushed his palm-leaf broom as if he were sweeping all his thoughts into a little mound for the wind to carry away.

At last he hung his broom on an iron hook, alongside an endless row of brooms, and went to the mare. Her stall door was closed so that the fragrance of late clover would not drift in to prick her appetite. He found her asleep, lying on her side, her great belly distended by the little colt soon to be born. Agba noticed, with a heavy feeling in his chest, that the fast was telling on the mare. He could read it in the sunken places above each eye, in the harshness of her coat.

But soon the fast would be over. It was the last day of the

month, and even now the sun was sinking below the gray-green olive trees that fringed the courtyard.

There was no sound anywhere, not from the palace walls beyond, nor from the quarters over the stables where the horseboys lived. The whole world seemed to be holding its breath, waiting for dusk to fall. Small voices of insects and birds were beginning to pierce the quiet. Twilight toads piping on their bassoons. Crickets chirping. Wood doves cooing. And afar off in the Atlas Mountains a hyena began to laugh. These were the forerunners of the darkness. It would be only a short time now.

Agba turned toward the east, his eyes on the minaret of the mosque. It was a sharp needle pricking the blood-red reflection of the sun. He gazed fixedly at it until his eyes smarted. At last a figure in white robes emerged from the tower. It was the public crier. He was sounding his trumpet. He was crying four times to the four winds of heaven. The fast of Ramadan was at an end!

The air went wild with noise. Twelve thousand horses recognized the summons and neighed their hunger. The royal stables seethed like an anthill. Horseboys swarmed out of the corridors and into the courtyard. From the hoods of their cloaks, from waistbands and vests, they took dates and raisins and almonds and popped them noisily into their mouths. They stripped the grapes from their vines. They ate with boisterous abandon. Some plunged their faces into the troughs and sucked the water as if they were horses.

Agba did not join the other horseboys. He returned to the mare. Moving slowly so as not to frighten her, he reached under the saddle hung on the wall and found the water vessel he had filled and hidden there an hour ago. He poured the water into a basin and waited for the mare to awaken.

As if she had heard in her dreams the sound made by the water, she woke with a jerk and struggled to her feet. She came to Agba and drank. Then she raised her head, letting the water slobber from her lips.

Agba waited motionless, knowing she would want more and more. Her deep brown eyes studied him as if to say, "You are the source of all that is good."

A great happiness welled up inside Agba. He nodded, seeming to understand her thoughts, then waited while she drank again and again.

When Agba came out of the mare's stall, the other boys were beginning to lead their horses to the common trough to drink. He must hurry now if he hoped to get his corn ration first. He picked up a bag made of hemp and ran through a maze of corridors and down a steep staircase to the underground granary. At the entrance stood Signor Achmet, Chief of the Grooms. Signor Achmet was dark and bearded. In his right hand he carried a knotted stick, and from the sash at his waist hung a hundred keys. When he saw Agba, he gripped the boy's shoulder with fingers as strong as the claws of an eagle.

"Why do you not eat with the other slaveboys?" he asked in his cracked voice. Then with a sharp look he released Agba and began peeling an orange with his fingernails. His beady eyes did not leave Agba's face as he ate the orange, making loud sucking noises to show how juicy and good it was.

Agba gulped. He studied his brown toes.

"Is it the mare?"

The boy's eyes flew to the Signor's.

"Is tonight her hour?"

Slowly, gravely, Agba nodded.

"Tonight, then," the Signor said, as he wiped his mouth on his mantle and began fumbling for the key to the granary, "tonight you will not go to your quarters to sleep. You will move the mare into the brood-mare stable. You will remain on watch and call me when she is ready to foal. The all-seeing eye of Allah will be upon you."

Agba's heart fluttered like bird wings. The Chief of the Grooms was letting him stay with his mare! He forgot all the cuffs and sharp words. He bowed low, impatient to hear the sound of the key turning the great lock, impatient for the creaking of the door and the mingled odors of corn and barley.

The key scraped. The door creaked open. The warm, mellow smells leaked out.

Signor Achmet stood aside. Agba slipped past him into the darkness. Quickly his sensitive fingers sought the good, sound ears of corn. He filled his bag with them. Then he turned and fled up the stairs.

But the mare would not eat the corn Agba brought. She only lipped it, then closed her eyes with a great weariness.

Agba was troubled as he watered and fed the other horses in his aisle, as he ate his own meal of barley and goat's milk, as he hurried to the brood-mare stable.

Signor Achmet must have been there before him. One of the stalls was wide open, and a lanthorn hung on a peg, sending out a feeble light. The stall had not been used since spring and had a fusty smell. Agba leaped upon the manger and threw open a tiny round window. It showed a patch of sky and the new moon.

"This is a favorable sign," he thought. "A new moon. A new month. The foal will be strong and swift." He took a deep breath of the cool summer night. Then quickly he went to work, filling bucket after bucket of sand from the huge sand pile behind the stables. Back and forth he ran, dumping the sand on the floor of the stall. Next he covered it with straw, spreading it out first with his hands, then trotting over it, galloping over it, around and around. At last he surveyed his work with approval. It would be a good bed for the mare!

Just as he was filling the manger with fodder, Signor

Achmet, in flowing white robes, looked in. He tested the depth of the sand with a bony forefinger. He felt the straw.

"You waste the sand and the straw," he said with a black look. "Half would do." But the Signor understood Agba's concern for the mare. "Fetch her now," he commanded.

Agba's bow was lost in the darkness.

"And you will summon me when she grows restless."

Swiftly and silently the Signor turned upon his heel, his white mantle fluttering behind him like moth wings.

The new moon hung over Agba's shoulder as he ran to get the mare. She was standing patiently in a corner of her stall, her head lowered, her tail tucked in. Placing a hand on her neck, Agba led her out into the night, past endless stalls and under endless archways to her new quarters. She walked slowly, heavily.

At the door of the new stall a tremor of fear shook her. She made a feeble attempt to go back, but Agba held her firmly, humming to hide his own nameless fears.

She entered the stall. She tried the soft bed with her feet. She went to the manger. Her nostrils widened to snuff the dried grasses, but she did not eat. She put her lips to the water cask but did not drink. At last she tucked her hooves underneath her and with a groan lay down. Her head nodded. She steadied it in the straw. Then her breathing, too, steadied.

As Agba stood on watch, his mind was a mill wheel, turning, turning, turning. He trembled, remembering the time he and the mare had come upon a gazelle, and he had ridden the mare alongside the gazelle, and she had outrun the wild thing. Agba could still feel the wind singing in his ears.

By closing his eyes he brought back the whole day. On the way home they had passed a wizened old storyteller in the streets, who, when Agba came near, motioned him close. The old man placed his hand on the mare's head. Then, in a voice that was no more than a whisper, he had said, "When

Allah created the horse, he said to the wind, 'I will that a creature proceed from thee. Condense thyself.' And the wind condensed itself, and the result was the horse."

The words danced in Agba's head as he watched the sleeping mare. *I will that a creature proceed from thee. Condense thyself! I will that a creature proceed from thee. Condense thyself!* He told the words over and over in his mind until suddenly the stable walls faded away and Agba was riding the South Wind. And there was nothing to stop him. No palace walls. No trees. Nor hedges. Nor rivers. Only white clouds to ride through, and a blue vaulted archway, and the wind for a mount.

With a sigh he sank down in the straw. His head dropped.

The boy's dreams spun themselves out until there was nothing left of them. He slept a deep sleep. The candle in the lanthorn sputtered and died. The new moon rode higher and higher. Bats and nighthawks, flying noiselessly in the velvet night, went about their business, swooping insects out of the air. With the gray light of morning they vanished, giving way to the jangling chorus of the crows.

Agba woke. The stable walls had closed in again. And there was the mare lying on her side as before. But her head was raised now, and she was drying off a newborn foal! Her tongue-strokes filled the silence of the stall, licking, licking, licking.

The boy watched in fear that if he took his eyes away the whole scene might vanish into the mist of the morning. Oh, how tiny the foal was! And so wet there was no telling what its color would be. But its eyes were open. And they were full of curiosity.

Agba's body quivered with the wonder of the little fellow's birth. He had seen newborn foals before, but none so small and finely made. In the distance he could hear the softly padding feet of the horseboys. He could hear the wild boar grunting and coughing in his hole behind the stables. He wondered if the boar really did keep evil spirits from entering into the horses.

Afraid to move, he watched the mare clumsily get to her feet. He watched her nudge the young thing with her nose.

The foal tried to get up. He thrust out his forefeet, but they splayed and he seemed to get all tangled up with himself. He tried again and again. For one breathless instant he was on his feet. Then his legs buckled and he fell in a little heap. Agba reached a hand toward him, but the mare came between. She pushed the little one with her nose. She pushed him with her tongue. She nickered to him. He was trying again. He was standing up. How spindly he was! And his ribs showed. And he had hollows above his eyes just like his dam.

"I could carry him in my arms," thought Agba. "He is not much bigger than a goat, and he has long whiskers like a goat. Long and silky. And his tail is curly. And he is all of one color. Except—except . . ." Suddenly the boy's heart missed a beat. On the off hind heel there was a white spot. It was no bigger than an almond, but it was there! The white spot—the emblem of swiftness!

Agba leaped to his feet. He wanted to climb the tower of the mosque. He wanted to blow on the trumpet. He wanted to cry to the four winds of heaven: "A foal is born. And he will be swift as the wind of the desert, for on his hind heel is a white spot. A white spot. A white . . ."

Just then a shaft of early sunlight pierced the window of the stable and found the colt. It flamed his coat into red gold. It made a sun halo around his head.

Agba was full of fear. He opened his mouth, but no sound escaped. Maybe this was all a dream. Maybe the foal was not real. The golden coat. The crown of sun rays. Maybe he was a golden horse belonging to the chariot of the sun!

"I'll capture him with a name," the boy thought quickly.

And he named the young thing Sham, which is the Arabic word for sun.

No sooner had Agba fastened a name on him than the little creature seemed to take on a new strength. He took a few steps. He found his mother's milk. He began to nurse, making soft sucking noises.

Agba knew he should be reporting to Signor Achmet. He knew he should be standing in line for his measure of corn. But he could not bear to break the spell. He listened to the colt suckling, to the mare munching the dried grasses. He smelled their warm bodies. A stable was a *good* place to be born.

P̃oet, novelist, biographer—Carl Sandburg was one of the most versatile and beloved of all American writers. His six-volume biography of Abraham Lincoln is considered one of the great works of American scholarship. But Sandburg also had a humorous side, which showed up in his delightful Rootabaga Tales.

The Rootabaga Tale that follows is whimsical, but also strangely haunting . . .

THE
White Horse Girl
AND THE
Blue Wind Boy

Carl Sandburg

When the dishes are washed at night time and the cool of the evening has come in summer or the lamps and fires are lit for the night in winter, then the fathers and mothers in the Rootabaga Country sometimes tell the young people the story of the White Horse Girl and the Blue Wind Boy.

The White Horse Girl grew up far in the west of the Rootabaga Country. All the years she grew up as a girl she liked to ride horses. Best of all things for her was to be straddle of a white horse loping with a loose bridle among the hills and along the rivers of the west Rootabaga Country.

She rode one horse white as snow, another horse white as new washed sheep wool, and another white as silver. And she could not tell because she did not know which of these three white horses she liked best.

"Snow is beautiful enough for me any time," she said, "new washed sheep wool, or silver out of a ribbon of the new moon, any or either is white enough for me. I like the white manes, the white flanks, the white noses, the white feet of all my ponies. I like the forelocks hanging down between the white ears of all three—my ponies."

And living neighbor to the White Horse Girl in the same prairie country, with the same black crows flying over their places, was the Blue Wind Boy. All the years he grew up as a boy he liked to walk with his feet in the dirt and the grass listening to the winds. Best of all things for him was to put on strong shoes and go hiking among the hills and along the rivers of the west Rootabaga Country, listening to the winds.

There was a blue wind of day time, starting sometimes six o'clock on a summer morning or eight o'clock on a winter morning. And there was a night wind with blue of summer stars in summer and blue of winter stars in winter. And there was yet another, a blue wind of the times between night and day, a blue dawn and evening wind. All three of these winds he liked so well he could not say which he liked best.

"The early morning wind is strong as the prairie and whatever I tell it I know it believes and remembers," he said, "and the night wind with the big dark curves of the night sky in it, the night wind gets inside of me and understands all my secrets. And the blue wind of the times between, in the dusk when it is neither night nor day, this is the wind that asks me questions and tells me to wait and it will bring me whatever I want."

Of course, it happened as it had to happen, the White Horse Girl and the Blue Wind Boy met. She, straddling one of her white horses, and he, wearing his strong hiking shoes

30

in the dirt and the grass, it had to happen they should meet among the hills and along the rivers of the west Rootabaga Country where they lived neighbors.

And of course, she told him all about the snow white horse and the horse white as new washed sheep wool and the horse white as a silver ribbon of the new moon. And he told her all about the blue winds he liked listening to, the early morning wind, the night sky wind, and the wind of the dusk between, the wind that asked him questions and told him to wait.

One day the two of them were gone. On the same day of the week the White Horse Girl and the Blue Wind Boy went away. And their fathers and mothers and sisters and brothers and uncles and aunts wondered about them and talked about them, because they didn't tell anybody beforehand they were going. Nobody at all knew beforehand or afterward why they were going away, the real honest why of it.

They left a short letter. It read:

To All Our Sweethearts, Old Folks and Young Folks:
We have started to go where the white horses come from and where the blue winds begin. Keep a corner in your hearts for us while we are gone.

The White Horse Girl.
The Blue Wind Boy.

That was all they had to guess by in the west Rootabaga Country, to guess and guess where two darlings had gone.

Many years passed. One day there came riding across the Rootabaga Country a Gray Man on Horseback. He looked like he had come a long ways. So they asked him the question they always asked of any rider who looked like he had come a long ways, "Did you ever see the White Horse Girl and the Blue Wind Boy?"

"Yes," he answered, "I saw them.

"It was a long, long ways from here I saw them," he went on, "it would take years and years to ride to where they are. They were sitting together and talking to each other, sometimes singing, in a place where the land runs high and tough rocks reach up. And they were looking out across water, blue water as far as the eye could see. And away far off the blue waters met the blue sky.

" 'Look!' said the Boy, 'that's where the blue winds begin.'

"And far out on the blue waters, just a little this side of where the blue winds begin, there were white manes, white flanks, white noses, white galloping feet.

" 'Look!' said the Girl, 'that's where the white horses come from.'

"And then nearer to the land came thousands in an hour, millions in a day, white horses, some white as snow, some like new washed sheep wool, some white as silver ribbons of the new moon.

"I asked them, 'Whose place is this?' They answered, 'It belongs to us; this is what we started for; this is where the white horses come from; this is where the blue winds begin.' "

And that was all the Gray Man on Horseback would tell the people of the west Rootabaga Country. That was all he knew, he said, and if there was any more he would tell it.

And the fathers and mothers and sisters and brothers and uncles and aunts of the White Horse Girl and the Blue Wind Boy wondered and talked often about whether the Gray Man on Horseback made up the story out of his head or whether it happened just like he told it.

Anyhow this is the story they tell sometimes to the young people of the west Rootabaga Country when the dishes are washed at night and the cool of the evening has come in summer or the lamps and fires are lit for the night in winter.

$\mathcal{P}$eter G. Roop was Wisconsin's "Teacher of the Year" for 1986–87. He has written over a dozen books—several of them with his wife, Connie. Their book Keep the Lights Burning, Abbie *was a Reading Rainbow Selection. Peter is fascinated by the history of the American Indians, and his research on their lives led to a series of stories that were so accurate they were adopted for use by the tribal council of the Montana Blackfeet Indians.*

Following is one of those stories.

$\mathcal{P}$ R A I R I E $\mathcal{L}$ I G H T N I N G

Peter G. Roop

Running Crane watched the last embers of the fire crumble into golden coals. Two Bows, the last of his grandfather's guests, had just left. Two Bows had been telling about the five strange animals he had seen in a Crow camp.

The boy sat by the old man, listening to the sounds of the Blackfeet camp as it settled down for the night. On a faraway butte a lonely wolf called for companionship.

"Come, my grandson," Naks'sa said. "It is time for you to sleep."

"But Naks'sa," protested Running Crane, "I want to hear once more about the elk-dogs."

"You heard what Two Bows said. And I have already told you all that I know of these unusual creatures."

"Then tell me again how large they are. Tell me what they

look like. Tell me how a man can climb on their backs and race the winds. Tell me, Naks'sa, please."

"Ha! Running Crane, you will have me talk the moon from the sky." The old man laughed and reached his wrinkled hands out toward the fire. "First you must put a few more sticks on the fire. Then I will tell you again about the elk-dogs."

Running Crane smiled as he quickly set several small branches on the glowing embers. The dry wood began to burn, filling the lodge with a yellow, dancing light.

Running Crane handed his grandfather his favorite pipe, an ancient pipe carved from a red stone in the shape of a buffalo. Naks'sa filled the buffalo bowl with tobacco.

"Now you know that I have never seen these elk-dogs. I have only heard about them from Two Bows and one other brave, Red Crow, chief of the Shoshoni."

The old man paused to pull a blazing stick from the fire. He lit his pipe, puffing out a long stream of gray smoke. Running Crane watched the smoke curl to the top of the tipi.

"These beasts are as big as the biggest elk," continued Naks'sa. "They are used by the white men to carry heavy burdens just as we use our dogs. They are both elk and dog. This is why we call them *poomkamita*, elk-dog. The elk-dog has long legs and can run like the wind over the prairie grass. But, most wondrous of all, Two Bows says that he has seen a Crow warrior climb on the back of an elk-dog and ride it as a small child rides on the back of a big dog!"

Running Crane stared at the fire. He saw images of elk-dogs in the blaze. And he saw himself on the back of the biggest elk-dog, running faster than a buffalo.

"These animals have hair all over their bodies. The longest hair is on their necks. They have long, straight tails that swing to the ground. But strangest of all is that no two elk-dogs are the same color."

36

Running Crane still stared at the elk-dog images in the fire. His elk-dog appeared black, as black as the heart of night.

"These elk-dogs eat grass like the buffalo," Naks'sa continued. "Two Bows said most are gentle and can be guided in any direction by a piece of rope looped through their mouths."

Running Crane gripped an imaginary rope tightly in his hands. He imagined riding his elk-dog wherever the swift wind went.

"Now, my young brave, it really is time for you to sleep."

Running Crane slowly left the lodge, his thoughts still filled with elk-dogs. Naks'sa watched him as he dropped the buffalo hide flap. The old man puffed on his pipe, knowing in his wisdom that these elk-dogs would change Running Crane, would change all of the Blackfeet people.

That change will be soon, Naks'sa thought as he put out his pipe.

The next morning Running Crane rose with the sun. He dashed from his lodge and plunged into the ice-cold river with all of the other Blackfeet boys. The chilly water chased the sleep from his eyes. He looked upstream at the Blackfeet warriors, the men of the tribe, bathing separately from the boys. *Someday, I will join them,* Running Crane said to himself.

"Kii! Running Crane," called Antelope, his cousin, as the boys stood dripping on the river bank. "After we have eaten, let us take our bows and hunt for birds in the cottonwoods downstream."

"No, not this morning, Antelope. I wish to stay in camp. I want to hear more talk about the elk-dogs. I think that the men are planning a raiding party against the Crows."

"Do you really think that we will steal some of those elk-dogs? The Crows have them and they are a strong people. They will not let us steal the elk-dogs without a fight."

"We will fight them if we must. Or we will trick them. Let us go hear what our fathers are saying."

The two young braves joined the men making arrows and mending bows. Running Crane's father, Strong Bear, was talking. Running Crane sat as close to his father as he could.

"It is a long march to the Crow camp," Strong Bear said. "We will be gone many days."

Running Crane felt his heart beat faster as a thought flashed into his head. Maybe he could join this raiding party. Maybe he could see real elk-dogs, not just his fire images.

"We must kill plenty of meat before we go," said Eagle Feather. "Our families must not be hungry while we are away."

"But we must hurry," Antelope's father, Seven Knives, added. "The Cold Maker will soon be here and snow will cover the ground."

"Then we will hunt today," Strong Bear said. "We leave for the Crow camp when the sun rises again."

Running Crane ached to ask his father if he could go on the raid, too. But he knew that he must wait to be asked to join the older braves on such a venture.

That afternoon Running Crane went hunting with his father. Each time his father said something about the raid on the Crow camp, Running Crane hoped he would ask him to go along. But Strong Bear did not.

Running Crane and Strong Bear walked far out onto the plains before they saw a small herd of grazing buffalo. They stayed downwind of the wary animals, crawling slowly closer so as not to stampede them. But an old bull saw them and began running. The rest of the herd thundered after him. Strong Bear and Running Crane watched the buffalo disappear over a distant hill.

"Grandfather says that an elk-dog can outrun a buffalo," Running Crane said.

"Did he tell you that men hunt buffalo while riding elk-dogs?"

"No," answered Running Crane, who was already imagining himself shooting an arrow from the back of his black elk-dog.

"With only a few elk-dogs, we could kill enough buffalo to feed the whole camp and never go hungry again," Strong Bear said. His words were intense and Running Crane looked hopefully at his father. But Strong Bear said nothing more.

On the way back to camp, Running Crane spotted some deer tracks. He knelt down to study them.

"Father, a deer has just passed here. It is heading toward those trees." Running Crane moved quickly along the tracks.

Strong Bear said nothing, but followed Running Crane as he stalked the deer.

Suddenly Running Crane held up his hand. Strong Bear stopped behind him. A deer grazed in an opening in the trees. Running Crane reached into his quiver and pulled out his best arrow. He notched the arrow, stretching the bow-string taut, then released it. The arrow flew straight but dropped short of the deer.

The deer looked in their direction. At that moment Running Crane heard the twang of his father's bow. The deer leaped up to run, then fell heavily.

Running Crane threw down his bow in disgust.

"That is not the way a warrior treats his bow," said Strong Bear.

"But this is a child's toy, not a warrior's bow," Running Crane muttered.

"Maybe the day will come when you earn a warrior's weapon," his father said. "Until that time, treat this bow with respect."

Running Crane picked up the bow and silently went to get his arrow.

Without another word Running Crane helped his father carry the deer to their lodge.

That night Running Crane risked his father's anger again. He could no longer hold back the question that had burned inside him all day.

"Father, may I join you on the raiding party? I am strong and can walk long distances. I won't complain. I will carry my own weapons and food." The words poured out like a rapidly running river.

Strong Bear looked at his son for a long time before answering.

"Can you be as silent as the owl in flight? Can you be as alert as the antelope? Can you be as cunning as the coyote?"

"Yes, Father, I can be all those things," answered Running Crane seriously.

"I have watched you grow from a small child to an almost-man. You can track and you can shoot straight. I think you are ready to join a raiding party. It is time for you to prove yourself to our people and to find your adult name. Yes, Running Crane, you may come with us to capture the elk-dogs."

As Strong Bear said these words, he looked at Running Crane's mother across the fire. She nodded her head slightly. She was smiling sadly when Running Crane looked at her.

"If you are joining the raiding party tomorrow, my son, then you must be off to bed now," she said.

"Please, may I go tell Grandfather?" Running Crane begged.

"Yes, but be quick. And don't ask him to tell you any more stories about the elk-dogs," his father said. "Your dreams are already filled with too many tales."

Running Crane dashed to Naks'sa's tipi. He yanked back the hide flap but lowered it slowly when he saw that his grandfather was asleep. When the boy had gone, the old man opened his eyes. A broad smile crossed Naks'sa's face as he got up and reached for his best quiver and arrows. He would wait until Running Crane slept before he placed them secretly beside the boy's buffalo robe bed.

It took Running Crane a long time to fall asleep that night. But when he finally did, his head filled with dreams. He dreamed of climbing on the broad back of his elk-dog. He dreamed of chasing a great buffalo and bringing it down with one arrow. He dreamed of racing the wind over the rippling prairie.

When he awoke, Running Crane saw the quiver and arrows. He was puzzled. At first he thought that his grandfather had accidentally left them. But he knew that Naks'sa had not hunted for years. Then he realized that his grandfather had known all along that he would be going on the raid.

One by one Running Crane pulled out each arrow and balanced it on his fingers. The shafts were straight, the points sharp. Naks'sa's spirit would go with him on his first raid.

As the warriors gathered, Running Crane was pleased to see Antelope standing beside his father. This would be Antelope's first raid, too. The boys hoped to return with many tales of their bravery to tell their friends.

The Blackfeet warriors traveled for five suns before reaching the land of the Crows. Each night they camped under the star-sprinkled sky. Each day they walked through canyons and along streams to avoid being seen by Crow scouts. On the fifth morning they climbed a high, steep hill. Running Crane hugged the ground with his companions as they spied on the Crow camp below.

The Crow lodges stood at the edge of a river. The camp was quiet. Women scraped hides and tended the many cooking fires. The men gathered in groups playing games or mending weapons. Children were scattered all over the camp, imitating the activities of their parents.

But Running Crane didn't care about what was happening in the camp. He wanted to see an elk-dog. His eyes searched

the camp for the strange beasts. All he saw were a few roam-
ing dogs.

"Where are the elk-dogs?" he whispered to Strong Bear.

His father pointed to an open grassy meadow downstream
from the lodges. Four elk-dogs, heads down, grazed on the
tall, sweet grass. A fifth elk-dog had a thick rope tied around
its neck. The rope was tied to a stake driven into the ground.
Running Crane wondered why only this elk-dog was tied.
The answer came soon.

Running Crane stared at the elk-dogs. They were just as his
grandfather had described them, only more beautiful than
Running Crane had imagined. They were larger than elks,
broader and taller. Their hair was long and each was indeed a
different color. Especially the one that was tied. That elk-dog
was jet black, blacker than the burned-out coals of a camp-
fire. Running Crane could not take his eyes off this elk-dog.
Bigger and stronger than any of the others, surely this creature could outrace the winds.

As Running Crane lay watching, a group of Crow braves
left the lodge circle and went to the elk-dogs. Four men
carried short ropes with loops in them. The men placed the
loops in the mouths of the four grazing elk-dogs and then
climbed on their backs. The black elk-dog was the only one
without a rope in its mouth.

One brave slowly approached the black elk-dog. A rope
dangled from one hand. He carried a thick branch in his
other hand. The man grabbed the rope around the elk-dog's
neck and yanked on it. The animal jerked its head away,
pawing the earth with its powerful front legs. Small clouds of
dust rose into the air.

The man stepped back quickly. The elk-dog tilted back its
head and made a strange sound. Never before had Running
Crane heard such a sound, such a mixture of anger and
strength.

Anger flooded through Running Crane. He reached into

his quiver for an arrow. He would kill the Crow before the man killed the elk-dog. As he pulled it out, he felt his father's hand grip the arrow.

"No, Running Crane," he said sternly, "we want to capture the elk-dogs. Do not give us away."

Running Crane let the arrow slip back into the quiver. He gritted his teeth to keep his anger in. It would be a worthy deed to steal the black elk-dog.

The man struck the elk-dog with the willow branch. The elk-dog reared, shaking his black mane and kicking at the Crow. The man hit the elk-dog on its back, then grabbed its neck. He struggled to get the other rope into the animal's mouth. When he finally did, the elk-dog reared again. The Crow brave held onto the ropes.

The brave tried to climb onto the elk-dog's back. Each time he got a leg up, the elk-dog reared, knocking the man to the ground. Finally the man gave up. He hit the elk-dog hard, threw down the stick, and walked away.

Running Crane ached to run down the hill and smash the Crow brave with the stick. He felt his father's hand on his shoulder. He stayed still.

The Blackfeet warriors watched the Crow camp all day. They watched the Crows ride the four gentle elk-dogs, turning them with the ropes in their mouths. They watched the men race the elk-dogs, circling the camps to the cheers of their friends. All of the elk-dogs were ridden except the black one.

As the sun rolled out of the sky and dropped behind the Backbone-of-the-World Mountains, the Blackfeet warriors made their plans for the raid that night.

"We will split into two groups," Strong Bear said. "One group will be led by Seven Knives. This group will attack the Crow camp, making as much noise as they can. The confusion will fool the Crows while the second group steals the elk-dogs."

"All of the elk-dogs?" Running Crane asked.

"No, we will not take the black elk-dog," said Strong Bear.

"But why?" asked Running Crane. "It is certainly the best of all of the elk-dogs."

Strong Bear looked at his son. "Because it is not gentle like the others. It would be bad medicine. Didn't you see how it attacked the Crow brave?"

"But he was hitting it," Running Crane said. "The man attacked the elk-dog first."

"We cannot risk anyone being injured. The other four elk-dogs are trained for riders. We will take only them."

"But," protested Running Crane.

Strong Bear's glaring eyes silenced him.

Running Crane was disappointed. The other elk-dogs were not nearly so magnificent as the black one. But he could not argue anymore against the decision of his elders. He knew, however, that someday, somehow, he would climb on that broad, black back and fly across the plains.

The Blackfeet raiders waited until thick, white clouds covered the moon, cutting off its silvery glow. Then they split up, Antelope going with the attacking warriors. Running Crane stayed with his father, with the group that would take the elk-dogs. Each warrior in this group had a rope wound tightly around his arm. The first four to reach the elk-dogs would place the ropes in their mouths and lead them away. The rest would stand watch and fight any Crows who appeared.

Strong Bear put his hand on Running Crane's arm. "If we are separated, head north. Keep the Backbone-of-the-World Mountains to your left. Do not follow our trail leading here. The Crow warriors may be watching it. In five days walk, turn toward the sun. Then you will find our camp."

Running Crane nodded his head.

"And remember to keep your bow away from the ground."

Running Crane gripped the bow tightly. His cheeks burned as he remembered the childish way he had cast his bow to the ground the previous day. "Yes, Father," he whispered.

It seemed like forever before Running Crane heard the hoot of an owl, the signal to attack. In the stillness of the night he heard the war cries of the other Blackfeet warriors as they rushed into the group camp.

Then, like shadows sliding down the hill, Running Crane and his companions ran to the elk-dogs. As the men approached, the elk-dogs made snorting noises, but they were easily captured. All but the black one. The braves ignored it as they rounded up the four elk-dogs and began leading them up the hill.

Running Crane hesitated, watching the great black elk-dog paw the ground. Without thinking he ran to it and reached out to touch the smooth coat. The animal shivered as the boy touched its flank, but it did not pull back. Running Crane whispered gently to the elk-dog as he ran his hands over the powerful shoulders. He set down his bow so that both hands could rub the silky coat.

Suddenly Running Crane heard a cry.

"Haiii!"

Running Crane spun in time to see a Crow warrior charging at him like a ghost from the night. Even in the dark he could see that it was the cruel owner of the black elk-dog, clutching a long knife in his hand.

Running Crane ducked as the blade flashed toward him. The blade slashed the night air, barely missing Running Crane. But as he turned to avoid the blade, Running Crane tripped and fell. The Crow warrior towered above him, an evil grin covering his face, the knife held high.

Just as Running Crane expected the knife to plunge through his heart, the black elk-dog reared, pulling the stake from the ground. Its hooves shot through the air, striking the

Crow a blow on the head. The man crashed down beside Running Crane with a thud. The frightened boy sucked in his breath, but the warrior lay dead on the grass.

Running Crane jumped up and ran to the elk-dog. The great black animal let the boy rub his face in the long hair on its neck. Then, slowly, as he whispered to the elk-dog, Running Crane gently took hold of the rope around the elk-dog's neck. Running Crane uncoiled the rope from his arm and put it in the animal's mouth. The elk-dog stood still.

Behind him Running Crane could hear more Crow warriors approaching. He frantically searched for his bow. Finally he found it. Without thinking he flung himself onto the elk-dog's broad back. The elk-dog shivered but did not throw the boy.

Running Crane turned the elk-dog as he had seen the Crows do with the other elk-dogs. He touched his heels to the smooth flanks as he had seen the Crows do when they raced. The great black elk-dog leaped forward.

Running Crane almost fell off. He gripped the elk-dog's thick mane and held on tightly. He adjusted his body, matching his movements to those of the elk-dog.

When Running Crane reached the top of the hill, he expected to meet his companions. But the top of the hill was empty. The raiders had already moved off into the night to escape the angry Crow warriors. He wondered if his father had thought he had been captured.

"Well, my friend," said Running Crane, "you saved my life tonight. Now we are left alone. Let us run far in the dark so that the Crows cannot find us. Then tomorrow we will ride to the home of your new people."

The elk-dog snorted, tossing its head. Running Crane touched his heels to the animal's flanks and the two disappeared into the night.

The boy and the elk-dog traveled until the moon set behind the mountains. Running Crane guided the elk-dog into a thicket of pine trees and tied the elk-dog to a small tree. Then the tired young Blackfeet warrior fell asleep on the soft bed of pine needles.

When Running Crane awoke, he took the elk-dog out into the tall prairie grass. The boy stood back and watched the animal snatch huge mouthfuls of grass and eat them. His own stomach growled and felt as empty as an old cooking pot. Yet before he would fill his stomach, Running Crane wanted to be farther from the Crows. He would hunt later. Running Crane felt the quiver on his back, the bow hung over his shoulders. He shivered, remembering that he had almost left his bow behind.

After the elk-dog had eaten his fill, Running Crane swung himself onto the animal. He patted the long, strong neck and said, "I will call you Pah-poom, the Blackfeet word for lightning. For even though you are as black as the night, you must be as fast as the jagged lightning."

Pah-poom bobbed his head as if he understood. Running Crane patted his neck again.

"Now let us see just how fast you can run!"

He kicked Pah-poom in the flanks. Like an arrow pulled to full bow, Pah-poom sped over the ground. Pah-poom's mane danced. The wind blew back Running Crane's black hair into a mane of his own. The boy balanced his weight and movements, rocking with each long stride.

On and on Pah-poom ran, rocketing up and down hills, splashing through streams. Once a herd of antelope, startled by their sudden appearance, sprang into motion. Prairie dogs disappeared under the ground as they neared.

The earth spun beneath Running Crane. He wondered if Pah-poom would ever stop running.

The big beast gradually slowed and began trotting again. Running Crane spoke gently to the elk-dog, pulling lightly on the rope. Pah-poom responded to his commands. Many times it seemed to the boy that it was Pah-poom teaching him. Running Crane wondered who had trained Pah-poom. Someone who had loved the animal. Certainly not the cruel, stick-swinging Crow warrior.

The two galloped, trotted, and cantered all day. Running Crane and Pah-poom stopped only twice during the long day to rest and drink from a stream. Pah-poom grazed at each stop, but Running Crane's stomach only growled louder. Still they kept going, although Running Crane knew they had come too far, too fast for the Crows to catch them even if they had more elk-dogs.

Toward sunset hunger got the best of Running Crane.

"Now we must find some food for me, Pah-poom. You can eat like the buffalo, but I, a Blackfeet warrior, must eat the buffalo."

They trotted up a long, rolling hill. Below on the other side Running Crane saw a herd of buffalo grazing on grass near a stream. It was a herd of cows and calves with a few bulls scattered among them.

Running Crane started to climb off Pah-poom's back to stalk the buffalo. Then he remembered Strong Bear's words about hunting buffalo from the backs of elk-dogs.

"Come, Pah-poom. You can run like the wind. Let us see if you can run like a buffalo!"

Running Crane pulled an arrow from his quiver and gripped his bow hard with his left hand. Then he kicked Pah-poom into action. The two streaked down the hill. The buffalo were too startled to move at first. Then one old bull began running and the rest charged after him. Running Crane kept his eyes on a small calf running at the rear of the herd.

"Go, Pah-poom! If you can catch that calf, I, too, will fill my stomach tonight," he shouted to the elk-dog as they thundered along. Pah-poom's hooves beat the earth with the rapid, heavy thump of a war drum.

Running Crane fit an arrow to his bow as the speeding elk-

dog caught up with the calf. The boy held on tightly with his knees while he pulled his bow back with all his strength. The arrow shot from the bow, hissing like a hornet. It flew straight, hitting the buffalo just below the shoulder. The calf stumbled, crashing to the ground.

Pah-poom turned and trotted back to the fallen buffalo. The calf wasn't dead, so Running Crane killed it quickly with his knife. He pulled his grandfather's arrow out, wiped it off on the grass, and slipped it back into the quiver.

"Thank you, Naks'sa," he whispered. "And thank you, Sun, for shining so brightly on my hunting."

That night, as he ate his eighth slice of buffalo meat, Running Crane knew that he had never tasted meat so good. Now he understood why his grandfather had always said, "No buffalo tastes as good as your first."

He already had plans for the soft calfskin. He would make a strong rope for Pah-poom. The rest he would give to his mother to make a new pair of moccasins for his grandfather.

In the morning, Running Crane finished skinning and butchering the buffalo. He made a large bag from the hide and loaded as much of the meat as he could onto the elk-dog's back.

"Pah-poom, you are more than an elk or a dog. You are strong medicine. You saved my life. You helped me kill my first buffalo. You make me feel like a man. You are a true friend of the Sun's."

The sun had reached the middle of the sky when Running Crane and Pah-poom rode into the Blackfeet camp. A great cry went up from all of the lodges. Friends and relatives stared at him astride the elk-dog. Running Crane rode the elk-dog to his grandfather's tipi.

"I have brought meat to your lodge, Grandfather," Running Crane said.

The old man gazed at the two for a long time.

Then he called in his loudest voice for a feast that night to celebrate the capture of the elk-dog and the return of his grandson.

Strong Bear's face broke into a great smile when he saw his son.

"Running Crane, we thought the Crows had captured you," Strong Bear said. "We reached camp only this morning. At sunrise tomorrow thirty braves were leaving to rescue you."

"How did you get back so fast?" Running Crane asked.

"We traveled day and night," answered Strong Bear. "I see you still carry your bow," he added proudly.

"Yes, Father," Running Crane said. "With it, I killed my first buffalo."

Naks'sa looked with pride at his grandson. He ducked into his lodge. He returned with his warrior's bow, a strong chokeberry wood bow, polished with age. Naks'sa handed the bow to Running Crane.

"Now that you have the heart of a Blackfeet warrior, you need a bow to match it," the old man said.

Running Crane shivered as he took the bow.

That night everyone feasted and rejoiced as the story of the raid was told. But no one in the lodge circle was as happy as Running Crane. He had ridden his first elk-dog and had raced the wind. He had returned safely from his first raid and had killed his first buffalo.

Pah-poom was strong medicine indeed.

Noted fantasy writer Jane Yolen has written more than a hundred books for children and adults; her picture book Owl Moon *received the prestigious Caldecott Award. In this poem she takes us back to prehistoric times for a look at the very first horse, Eohippus, who would one day become partner to another mammal, a species known as* humans.

DAWN HORSE

The sea lays down its sandy bed
Imprinting bone and horn and head
Of dinosaurs that are long dead.
    While near the prehistoric lakes
    Where mammal its new thirst now slakes
    Dawn Horse awakes.
On each front foot there are four toes.
It has a blunt, unseemly nose.
Eyes in the front watch where it goes.
    Now browsing forth, its food it takes.
    We do not know the sound it makes.
    Dawn Horse awakes.
A million years have come and gone
Since Eohippus galloped on
From that most green and ancient dawn.
    Till now, next every step we take,
    Proud horses prancing hoofprints make.
    Not only did Dawn Horse awake
            In that old Eocene.

—Jane Yolen

$\mathcal{A}$nne Eliot Crompton is a New England-based writer who has created many memorable horse stories, including the popular book The Rain Cloud Pony. Here she turns her imagination back to a time that has always fascinated her, the time of the cave dwellers . . .

$\mathcal{W}$ HITE $\mathcal{H}$ ORSES

Anne Eliot Crompton

That morning on Magic Mountain I was young. I bounded like a Goat down the Mountain and ran among the People's tents to my mother's tent. I grabbed the front tent pole and hung there, panting. I gasped, "I met a fanged Cat!"

Mother looked up from nursing Baby.

Too late I saw that the Peoples' Aunt sat beside her, cross-legged on our old, worn Bison robe. I had interrupted my mother and the Aunt in serious conversation, but I was too excited—frightened—to apologize. I gabbled, "Cat! Fanged Cat!"

Slowly, the Aunt looked up at me.

In her white hair that was once sunny-bright, she wore strings of Cave Bear teeth. Her skinny neck and arms and legs were wound with claws, shells, and Cat fangs. All these ornaments gleamed in the morning Sun, but her old eyes gleamed sharper. Those eyes that saw Spirits looked through me, saw where I had been, what I had done. Quietly, as though she did not know the answer, the Aunt asked me, "Why did you go up Magic Mountain, past the Cave?" I saw that she wanted my mother to know.

Bravely I said, "I went up on a Dream Quest."

The Aunt turned to my mother, and their eyes met. Then she turned back to me. Gently she said, "You will be Woman. You have no need to dream."

Soon I would be Woman, magical as Earth Herself. I needed no dream of Cat, Bird, or Serpent to tell me who or what I was. But I told the Aunt, "I have dreamed. If it was a dream. It seemed real."

The piercing eyes looked through me. The hooked nose wrinkled. "Cat really happened. You smell of Cat. Tell us."

"Cat was close." Remembering, I seemed to look down his gullet again and hear his silent steps. I broke out in sweat.

The Aunt nodded. One bony hand patted the robe beside her. "Tell us."

Trembling, I sank down knee to knee with the Aunt. Haltingly at first, I told my story. My words were simple, but as I spoke them I lived the story again.

I said, "Last night I climbed Magic Mountain by Moonlight."

And I remembered climbing the trail past the black mouth of Magic Cave. During the Summer Gathering boys go in there and dream for three days and nights. At dawn on the fourth day they come out as men. Being female, and having no need of dreams, I would never go there. But I wanted to go! I wanted to dream like a boy! In my head and hands I had a special gift that made me want, need, to dream.

Climbing past the Cave, I heard a drumbeat deep in the Mountain. The Peoples' Uncles were casting a hunting spell down there. Maybe the Aunt was with them. She went there, even though she was female, because she had the gift of Magic. Maybe she beat the drum that said, *Come.*

Resisting the call, I climbed higher. Near the top I sat against a boulder and watched the full Moon sink. There I waited for a dream, a vision, a happening to change my life.

As the dawn lightened, the Summer Gathering of the People appeared below me. Tents leaned together, shared fires glowed as women stirred coals. Children raced among the tents and out into the flowered plain. On the very far horizon —too far to be seen from down there—a brown herd moved very, very slowly. I stood up to see better. Those swaying, swinging animals were Mammoths! The drum had called them.

In my grandmother's time Mammoths often came to the drum's call. The People drove herds of them off cliffs with torches. My grandmother had waved a torch in the front line. Tough tents were made from Mammoth hide, magic figures were carved from tusk, the People ate richly. But lately the charms and spells that draw Mammoth Spirits into the World had failed, and Mammoth was rare. I stared as the herd ambled across the horizon. This would indeed be a special day!

I felt the drum's call in my bones, as the Mammoths felt it in their plodding feet. *Come,* said the drum. I longed to enter the Cave, but I must not. I climbed higher.

There is a trail over the top if you can find it. I had played on Magic Mountain as a child, through many Summer Gatherings. My feet found the narrow, hidden trail between boulders. Before Sunrise I passed, panting, over the top, and left our Cave and plain behind.

On the other side wrinkled hills roll away, pierced by long valleys. In the valley under me a Horse family grazed.

I crept out on a ledge and peered down. Never had I seen such Horses before.

They were white. The growing light showed yellow-brown freckles on their coats, but at first glance they were simply white. A voice in my mind whispered that I had heard tell of white Horses. Some story, some old song described them. They were larger, sleeker than the bristly brown horses we hunted. Two mares and a yearling grazed just beyond spearthrow. My hand crept to the knife in my belt. They were rich meat! Unless . . . unless they were spirit Horses. Closer, a movement caught my eye.

The stallion grazed directly below me. He was pure white, white as windflowers. He moved over dewy grass like a ghost, shaking mane, swishing tail, cropping flowers. Beside him a crevice opened into the cliff.

Silently I scrabbled about on the rock to peer into the crevice. The rising Sun peered in, too.

In the crevice a pure white mare nursed her pure white foal.

The stallion guarded the entrance. The family waited nearby. The foal had been born in the night. His birth cord dangled, his legs wobbled. He nursed eagerly, switching his fluff-tail. Spirit Horses do not give birth, do they?

Watching, I held my breath. No wind warned the Horses of my presence. If I made no sound, I could watch them all day.

I wanted to draw them. Picture-making was my gift. If I had found a stick to hand, and soft earth, I would have drawn the curves of backs and sides, the prick of ears. I wanted to carve them on horn or bone, to bewitch a hunter's spear. I decided to memorize them and draw them later.

I do not know why I raised my eyes, what warned me. I looked up to see the fanged Cat approaching across the crevice.

He flowed between the boulders like a great brown serpent. Twice my size, he had many times my power. I saw it in his bunched shoulders and tense hindquarters. He slunk to the cliff edge across from me and peered down. He grinned, and his tail swept the rocks. Rising sunshine glinted off his fangs. His stink came over me like a cloud, and stuck my tongue to the roof of my mouth.

He could leap across at me, or down upon the white foal.

If I did not move, he might not notice me.

Grinning, silent, he crouched to fall upon the foal. Or the

mare. I could see that thought behind his yellow eyes: Deal with the mare first; she could kick.

Spirit Horses do not give birth. Those were meat-and-bone horses down there. Meat and bone I had seen before, but never horses white as windflowers. These horses were meat and bone—but they were also magic, rare in the world as walking Fish, or talking Birds.

My feet scrabbled stone and pushed me up.

My voice yelled.

My hand grabbed the knife from my belt and hurled it at Cat.

The knife struck rock and bounced into the crevice.

Teetering on the cliff edge, I faced Cat.

Crouched to spring, he snarled up at me. I looked past his gleaming fangs down his red gullet.

Below us, hooves clashed on rock. Without looking, I knew that the white stallion galloped into the crevice. My eyes never left Cat's yellow glare.

Cat shrank back a step, belly to rock.

He did not know I was unarmed. He did not know I was young and female. But he knew I was human.

The Uncles say that Cat, Bear, and Wolf all fear humans. I know that this is true, because I saw it that morning on Magic Mountain. I stared into Cat's eyes while he drew back another slow, silent step.

Undecided, he trembled. His powerful shoulders shook; the rich brown hide crawled on his stretched muscles. Would he attack me? (I knew that he would not.) Would he attack the white horses? He glanced down.

I glanced down.

Mare and stallion reared up and snapped yellow teeth at Cat. The rocks rang with their angry screams.

I looked up. Cat was gone.

Now the stallion bared his teeth at me. Cat out of sight, I

was the enemy. I drew back from the edge so that I no longer seemed poised to leap on the foal.

The stallion turned on the mare. With nips, pushes, and shoves he drove her and the foal below me and out of the crevice. The foal stumbled and reeled. Once he sprawled on the rocks, but the stallion urged him up and out of that dangerous crevice.

Heads high, ears forward, the three freckled horses waited in the open valley. They had heard the screams, snarls, and my yelling. But they knew themselves safe in the open. They trusted to each other, and to their hooves, heels, and teeth. The pure white mare and foal tottered into their midst. Alert between them and the crevice, the stallion watched me.

I called to him, "I'm going away now. Cat is gone." Ah, but how far?

I had lost a good knife down that crevice, but I wasn't going after it. Once more I looked at the white horses standing hock-deep in grass and flowers. Once more I looked at the foal I had saved. Wherever in the world he galloped, he would take part of my spirit with him.

Again I called to the stallion, "Look now, I'm going away. Watch me." The stallion snorted. He thought he had frightened me away, and I let him think so.

I turned and made my way between boulders toward the pass. At every step I expected Cat to bound out of shadow or over a rock. He could not fall on me from above, for I was the highest thing on Magic Mountain. I walked firmly, trusting in my humanness, armed only with humanness. I came over the pass and saw the Summer Gathering below, leaning tents and shared fires, children playing, men leaving on a hunt. On the far horizon the Bison herd had lain down to chew cud in the strong morning light.

I glanced back at the rocky pass I had just come through. Shadows seemed to slink. I almost heard the pad of perfectly silent paws.

I bounded down the slope like a mountain Goat and ran straight to my mother's tent. I grabbed the tent pole and hung there, panting. I gasped, "I met a fanged Cat!"

Mother and the Aunt heard my story. My words were too simple, I could not describe what I had seen. I stumbled in the telling, as the foal had stumbled on the rocks. Unspeaking, the Aunt handed me the knife from her belt. I pushed the Bison robe aside and drew pictures on hard earth with the knife. In this way I showed them the faltering foal, creeping Cat, myself on the cliff edge, facing Cat.

The story ended, pictures drawn, I sat on the robe knee to knee with the Aunt. I no longer trembled. Telling the tale had drained the dread from it. I no longer looked down Cat's gullet or heard his silent step. I sat there, thin and light and not yet Woman. But my story was true.

The Aunt and my mother looked at each other. I saw then that they had talked about me, earlier. The Aunt's gaze said: *What did I tell you!*

Mother looked away. Then she bent over Baby, asleep now in her lap, and the Aunt turned back to me.

She said, "Horses white as windflowers appear now and then, here and there. You have heard of them."

"Maybe. Some song or story."

"They appear to Aunts and Uncles, Spirit people, and to those who will be Spirit people."

Her eyes were grave as her voice. Frightened again, I shivered.

She said, "I have watched you since you drew your first picture in riverbank mud. It was a Fish picture. Picture-making is Magic-making."

I drew a deep breath. I must have always known it. Why else had I gone up Magic Mountain to dream?

Later, the Aunt led me into the twisting passages of Magic Mountain. We crawled, squeezed, and climbed into Magic Cave, where painted Bison gallop across rock walls. Painted

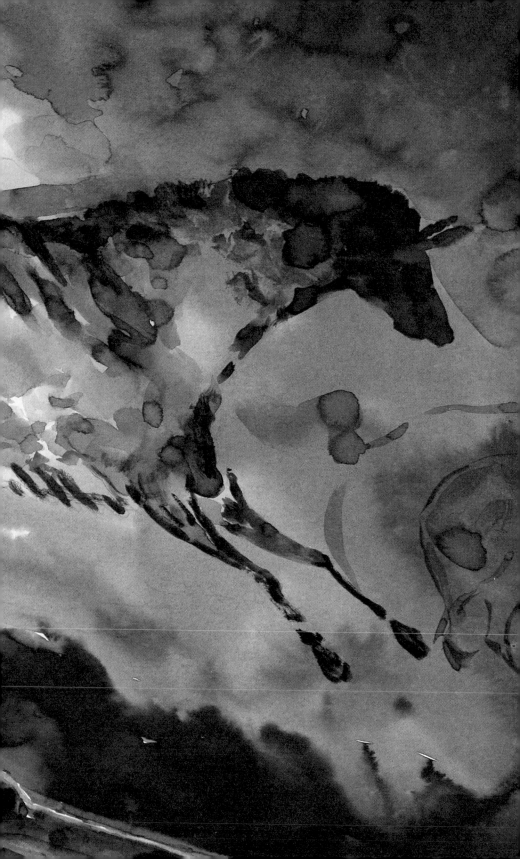

Reindeer swim here, holding heavy antlers high. Bristly brown Horses stand alert. Under these new paintings one can see old Mammoth pictures, which have lost their power.

I stared amazed at the paintings, which flickered with life in our torchlight. I seemed to hear the thunder of hooves and Horses neighing. Never had I guessed what wonders paint could create!

Not yet Woman, I crawled under a rock overhang and drew my mare and foal on the rock above, where only caring eyes would find them. Since then, each time I crawl, squeeze, and climb into Magic Cave, I go first to that overhang. I lie down, look up, and remember.

That long-ago morning on Magic Mountain I was young. Now I am old. I have been Woman, Mother, Peoples' Aunt. I have worked healing spells and hunting spells. My drum has called Reindeer, Bison, and brown bristly Horses to the People. One time it called Mammoth. I have walked with Fish and talked with Birds.

But never since that morning have I seen Horses white as windflowers.

*Alexander the Great was one of the most remarkable
figures in all of history—a warrior who overcame most of the
known world, who is said to have wept when there were no
more kingdoms to conquer, who left his mark on civilizations
from Egypt to India. In the story that follows, Alexander—
still a boy—meets for the first time the great horse that would
accompany him for much of his brilliant career.*

THE

*T*AMING

OF

*B*UCEPHALUS

Retold by Bruce Coville

The boy stood with his back to hot afternoon sun, his
shadow stretching before him. Though he was only of medium height, he was well muscled and carried himself with a
regal air. Clearly he was born to command—though looking
at him now, one might not suspect that when he became a
man he would write his name across the world as the greatest
conqueror of all time.

His name was Alexander, and he was watching his father's
men battle the most powerful horse he had ever seen.

They had been working for over an hour with little suc-
cess. The horse, which was so black its coat seemed to swal-

low the light, bucked and reared and plunged with increasing frenzy as the men tried to ride it. Clouds of dust filled the still afternoon air as the horse's great hooves pounded against the earth.

"Enough!" cried a sharp voice.

Alexander looked to his right. His father, King Philip of Macedon, looked angry. Alexander wasn't surprised. He knew that his father had paid a huge sum of money for this magnificent horse. Now it appeared that money had been wasted.

"I have never seen such an obstinate beast," muttered the king. "Bull-headed through and through."

Alexander smiled. With his great broad head, the horse might well be named Bucephalus, or bull head.

But the boy's smile faded as he heard his father's next words: "Take him back. We have no room for such a temper in my army. Sell him for whatever you can find."

Alexander was appalled. This huge horse was the most magnificent animal he had ever seen. To lose him because those fools could not ride him was unthinkable.

"Father, wait," he said, striding to where Philip had stood watching the attempts to ride Bucephalus.

Philip turned his one good eye to the boy. Though he was still angry, his face softened, for there was nothing in the world that he loved as he loved his son.

"Wait for what?" he asked.

"We can't let the horse go. We'll never see his like again."

"May we never see the like of his temper again," said Philip bitterly. "I don't believe there's a man alive who can ride him."

Alexander refrained from mentioning that the horse's wild temper was not that different from his father's. Plunging on, he said, "I can ride him."

Philip's snort was not unlike the sounds made by the great horse. "Alexander," he said, "you are a prince. One day you

will be King. But you are not a god, and you would do well to remember that. The best riders in my army have tried and failed. Why do you think you can do any better?"

"Because they have used only muscles and not their brains," said Alexander simply. "Because they think like soldiers, and I think like a king."

Philip sighed. Alexander's self-assurance was a matter of some concern to him. Many of his soldiers still resented the afternoon at the festival of games when Alexander had declined to join the footraces. "The other runners are only men," he had said. "I will race only with kings."

Maybe it would do the boy good to try and fail at something.

"All right," said Philip grudgingly. "You can try."

"And if I succeed, will he be mine?" asked Alexander.

"If you want to bargain like a man," said Philip, looking at his son shrewdly, "then you must take risks like a man. I agree: if you succeed, the bull head will be yours. But if you fail, then you must pay me his full price. Do you still want to try?"

Philip expected his son to hesitate for at least a moment. The price of Bucephalus would put a mortgage on the boy's future that would tie him down for years. And Alexander knew his father would not simply forget the matter. That was not the way you raised a king, and Philip and Alexander both knew it.

But the boy's answer was instant and positive: "I accept the challenge."

For an instant Philip seemed to feel the hand of destiny. What was this boy he had fathered, that he could take such a risk without a sign of flinching? He watched with mixed emotions as Alexander walked across the dusty corral to where the horse stood waiting, its flanks quivering, its nostrils wide. The sun was at its back. Stretching from its feet was a shadow so black it looked like an extension of the horse, making its body appear even more massive.

Alexander walked slowly, to let the horse grow accustomed to his approach. The animal, wild-eyed and ready to rear, seemed to tower above him.

"Ho, Bucephalus," crooned the boy. "You have nothing to fear from me. But I know what you *do* fear."

Dropping his voice so that the others could not hear, Alexander continued to whisper to the horse. "That shadow makes you frightened, does it not?"

For Alexander, standing and watching, had seen what the soldiers and riders had ignored. That Bucephalus was indeed afraid of the huge black shadow that stretched before him in the afternoon sun, a shadow that became all the more terrifying whenever Bucephalus bucked and reared, for then it looked as if the black horse on the ground was trying to strike back at him.

"Slowly," said Alexander, "gently, great heart, let us see the sun."

Taking the lead rope, he turned Bucephalus so that the great head was facing directly toward the sun, and his shadow fell behind him.

"Now," said Alexander, "now you see the shadow is gone, and there is nothing to fear."

The horse didn't move. Reaching out, Alexander placed one hand against the animal's neck.

And in that instant of their first contact the horse quivered, and Alexander quivered, and the world seemed to spin black around them. A sudden vision overwhelmed the boy—a vision of himself astride Bucephalus, and Bucephalus astride the world itself. And in that moment he understood that this was the horse he would ride to glory, the key to the greatness he had always known lay ahead for him.

Swinging one leg up, Alexander pulled himself into position on the horse's back.

Bucephalus snorted and pawed the earth nervously. But there was no shadow to paw back, so he did not plunge and rear as the observers expected.

A whisper rippled through the men standing around the fence. But the murmur of words never reached the King, for Philip was lost in wonder. Standing by himself, he watched as his son urged the great black horse into a walk, then a trot, and finally a thundering gallop. For a moment he thought his heart would burst with pride. Then a sudden shout of triumph burst from his lips. "Ride, Alexander!" he cried. "Ride!"

And now, at last, tamed by a heart greater than his own, Bucephalus knew no fear. With Alexander on his back, the great horse hurtled forward. Together, they raced out of the afternoon sun, into a world that would never be large enough to hold them.

When Anna Sewell started Black Beauty *in the early 1870s, it is unlikely she had any idea of what a sensation her book would create. The gentle Quaker woman, who had been crippled from the time she was twelve, felt a need to show the world how cruelly horses were often treated by the men they served. And what better way to do it than by telling the story from the point of view of the horse?*

The book was published in 1877. Although Anna Sewell had sold the book to her publisher for a flat fee of twenty pounds and never received any royalties on her bestselling work, she did have the satisfaction of seeing it become an important tool in the worldwide battle against cruelty to animals.

In this selection, a young lad named Joe Green is assigned to take care of Beauty. But Joe is inexperienced in the ways of horses, and from that inexperience comes disaster.

JOE GREEN GROWS UP

Anna Sewell

(from *Black Beauty*)

One night after I had eaten my hay and was lying down in my straw fast asleep, I was suddenly roused by the stable bell ringing very loud. I heard the door of John's house open, and his feet running up to the hall. He was back again in no time; he unlocked the stable door, and came in, calling out, "Wake up, Beauty! You must go well now, if ever you did," and almost before I could think he had got the saddle on my back

71

and the bridle on my head. He ran around for his coat, and then took me at a quick trot up to the hall door. The squire stood there, with a lamp in his hand.

"Now, John," he said, "ride for your life—that is, for your mistress's life; there is not a moment to lose. Give this note to Dr. White; give your horse a rest at the inn, and be back as soon as you can."

John said, "Yes, sir," and was on my back in a minute. The gardener who lived at the lodge had heard the bell ring, and was ready with the gate open, and away we went through the park, and through the village, and down the hill till we came to the tollgate. John called very loud and thumped upon the door; the man was soon out and flung open the gate.

"Now," said John, "do you keep the gate open for the doctor; here's the money," and off he went again.

There was before us a long piece of level road by the riverside; John said to me, "Now, Beauty, do your best," and so I did; I wanted no whip nor spur, and for two miles I galloped as fast as I could lay my feet to the ground; I don't believe that my old grandfather, who won the race at Newmarket, could have gone faster. When we came to the bridge John pulled me up a little and patted my neck. "Well done, Beauty! good old fellow," he said. He would have let me go slower, but my spirit was up, and I was off again as fast as before. The air was frosty, the moon was bright; it was very pleasant. We came through a village, then through a dark wood, then uphill, then downhill, till after eight miles' run we came to the town, through the streets and into the marketplace. It was all quite still except the clatter of my feet on the stones—everybody was asleep. The church clock struck three as we drew up at Dr. White's door. John rang the bell twice, and then knocked at the door like thunder. A window was thrown up, and Dr. White, in his nightcap, put his head out and said, "What do you want?"

"Mrs. Gordon is very ill, sir; master wants you to go at once; he thinks she will die if you cannot get there. Here is a note."

"Wait," he said, "I will come."

He shut the window and was soon at the door.

"The worst of it is," he said, "that my horse has been out all day and is quite done up; my son has just been sent for, and he has taken the other. What is to be done? Can I have your horse?"

"He has come at a gallop nearly all the way, sir, and I was to give him a rest here; but I think my master would not be against it, if you think fit, sir."

"All right," he said, "I will soon be ready."

John stood by me and stroked my neck; I was very hot. The doctor came out with his riding whip.

"You need not take that, sir," said John. "Black Beauty will go till he drops. Take care of him, sir, if you can; I should not like any harm to come to him."

"No, no, John," said the doctor, "I hope not," and in a minute we had left John far behind.

I will not tell you about our way back. The doctor was a heavier man than John, and not so good a rider; however, I did my very best. The man at the tollgate had it open. When we came to the hill the doctor drew me up. "Now, my good fellow," he said, "take some breath." I was glad he did, for I was nearly spent, but that breathing helped me on, and soon we were in the park. Joe was at the lodge gate; my master was at the hall door, for he had heard us coming. He spoke not a word; the doctor went into the house with him, and Joe led me to the stable. I was glad to get home; my legs shook under me, and I could only stand and pant. I had not a dry hair on my body, the water ran down my legs, and I steamed all over, Joe used to say, like a pot on fire. Poor Joe! he was young and small, and as yet he knew very little, and his father, who would have helped him, had been sent to the next village; but I am sure he did the very best he knew. He

rubbed my legs and my chest, but he did not put my warm cloth on me; he thought I was so hot I should not like it. Then he gave me a pailful of water to drink; it was cold and very good, and I drank it all; then he gave me some hay and some corn, and thinking he had done right, he went away. Soon I began to shake and tremble, and turned deadly cold; my legs ached, my loins ached, and my chest ached, and I felt sore all over. Oh! how I wished for my warm, thick cloth, as I stood and trembled. I wished for John, but he had eight miles to walk, so I lay down in my straw and tried to go to sleep. After a long while I heard John at the door; I gave a low moan, for I was in great pain. He was at my side in a moment, stooping down by me. I could not tell him how I felt, but he seemed to know it all; he covered me up with two or three warm cloths, and then ran to the house for some hot water; he made me some warm gruel, which I drank, and then I think I went to sleep.

John seemed to be very much put out. I heard him say to himself over and over again, "Stupid boy! stupid boy! no cloth put on, and I dare say the water was cold, too; boys are no good," but Joe was a good boy after all.

I was now very ill; a strong inflammation had attacked my lungs, and I could not draw my breath without pain. John nursed me night and day; he would get up two or three times in the night to come to me. My master, too, often came to see me. "My poor Beauty," he said one day, "my good horse, you saved your mistress's life, Beauty; yes, you saved her life." I was very glad to hear that, for it seems the doctor had said if we had been a little longer it would have been too late. John told my master he never saw a horse go so fast in his life. It seemed as if the horse knew what was the matter. Of course I did, though John thought not; at least I knew as much as this —that John and I must go at the top of our speed, and that it was for the sake of the mistress.

I do not know how long I was ill. Mr. Bond, the horse doctor, came every day. One day he bled me; John held a pail for the blood. I felt very faint after it and thought I should die, and I believe they all thought so too.

Ginger and Merrylegs had been moved into the other stable, so that I might be quiet, for the fever made me very quick of hearing; any little noise seemed quite loud, and I could tell everyone's footstep going to and from the house. I knew all that was going on. One night John had to give me a draught; Joe's father, Thomas Green, came in to help him. After I had taken it and John had made me as comfortable as he could, he said he should stay half an hour to see how the medicine settled. Thomas said he would stay with him, so they went and sat down on a bench that had been brought into Merrylegs' stall, and put down the lantern at their feet, that I might not be disturbed with the light.

For a while both men sat silent, and then Tom Green said in a low voice:

"I wish, John, you'd say a bit of a kind word to Joe. The boy is quite broken-hearted; he can't eat his meals, and he can't smile. He says he knows it was all his fault, though he is sure he did the best he knew, and he says if Beauty dies no one will ever speak to him again. It goes to my heart to hear him. I think you might give him just a word; he is not a bad boy."

After a short pause John said slowly, "You must not be too hard upon me, Tom. I know he meant no harm, I never said he did; I know he is not a bad boy. But you see, I am sore myself; that horse is the pride of my heart, to say nothing of his being such a favorite with the master and mistress; and to think that his life may be flung away in this manner is more than I can bear. But if you think I am hard on the boy I will try to give him a good word tomorrow—that is, I mean if Beauty is better."

"Well, John, thank you. I knew you did not wish to be too hard, and I am glad you see it was only ignorance."

John's voice almost startled me as he answered:

"Only ignorance! only ignorance! how can you talk about only ignorance? Don't you know that it is the worst thing in the world, next to wickedness?—and which does the most mischief heaven only knows. If people can say, 'Oh! I did not know, I did not mean any harm,' they think it is all right. I suppose Martha Mulwash did not mean to kill that baby when she dosed it with Dalby and soothing syrups; but she did kill it, and was tried for manslaughter."

"And serve her right, too," said Tom. "A woman should not undertake to nurse a tender little child without knowing what is good and what is bad for it."

"Bill Starkey," continued John, "did not mean to frighten his brother into fits when he dressed up like a ghost and ran after him in the moonlight; but he did; and that bright, handsome little fellow, who might have been the pride of any mother's heart, is just no better than an idiot, and never will be, if he lives to be eighty years old. You were a good deal cut up yourself, Tom, two weeks ago, when those young ladies left your hothouse door open, with a frosty east wind blowing right in; you said it killed a good many of your plants."

"A good many!" said Tom. "There was not one of the tender cuttings that was not nipped off. I shall have to strike all over again, and the worst of it is that I don't know where to go to get fresh ones. I was nearly mad when I came in and saw what was done."

"And yet," said John, "I am sure the young ladies did not mean it; it was only ignorance."

I heard no more of this conversation, for the medicine did well and sent me to sleep, and in the morning I felt much better; but I often thought of John's words when I came to know more of the world.

Joe Green went on very well; he learned quickly, and was so attentive and careful that John began to trust him in many things; but as I have said, he was small of his age, and it was seldom that he was allowed to exercise either Ginger or me; but it so happened one morning that John was out, and the master wanted a note to be taken immediately to a gentleman's house, about three miles distant, and sent his orders for Joe to saddle me and take it, adding the caution that he was to ride steadily.

The note was delivered, and we were quietly returning when we came to the brickfield. Here we saw a cart heavily laden with bricks; the wheels had stuck fast in the stiff mud of some deep ruts, and the carter was shouting and flogging the two horses unmercifully. Joe pulled up. It was a sad sight. There were the two horses straining and struggling with all their might to drag the cart out, but they could not move it; the sweat streamed from their legs and flanks, their sides heaved, and every muscle was strained, while the man, fiercely pulling at the head of the fore horse, swore and lashed most brutally.

"Hold hard," said Joe, "don't go on flogging the horses like that; the wheels are so stuck that they cannot move the cart."

The man took no heed, but went on lashing.

"Stop! pray stop!" said Joe. "I'll help you to lighten the cart; they can't move it now."

"Mind your business, you impudent young rascal, and I'll mind mine!" The man was in a towering passion and the worse for drink, and laid on the whip again. Joe turned my head, and the next moment we were going at a round gallop toward the house of the master brickmaker. I cannot say if John would have approved of our pace, but Joe and I were both of one mind, and so angry that we could not have gone slower.

The house stood close by the roadside. Joe knocked at the door, and shouted, "Halloo! Is Mr. Clay at home?" The door was opened, and Mr. Clay himself came out.

"Halloo, young man! You seem in a hurry; any orders from the squire this morning?"

"No, Mr. Clay, but there's a fellow in your brickyard flogging two horses to death. I told him to stop, and he wouldn't; I said I'd help him to lighten the cart, and he wouldn't, so I have come to tell you. Pray, sir, go." Joe's voice shook with excitement.

"Thank ye, my lad," said the man, running in for his hat; then pausing for a moment—"Will you give evidence of what you saw if I should bring the fellow up before a magistrate?"

"That I will," said Joe, "and gladly, too." The man was gone, and we were on our way home at a smart trot.

"Why, what's the matter with you, Joe? You look angry all over," said John, as the boy flung himself from the saddle.

"I am angry all over, I can tell you," said the boy, and then in hurried, excited words he told all that had happened. Joe was usually such a quiet, gentle little fellow that it was wonderful to see him so roused.

"Right, Joe! you did right, my boy, whether the fellow gets a summons or not. Many folks would have ridden by and said it was not their business to interfere. Now I say that with cruelty and oppression it is everybody's business to interfere when they see it; you did right, my boy."

Joe was quite calm by this time, and proud that John approved of him, and he cleaned out my feet and rubbed me down with a firmer hand than usual.

They were just going home to dinner when the footman came down to the stable to say that Joe was wanted directly in master's private room; there was a man brought up for ill-using horses, and Joe's evidence was wanted. The boy flushed

up to his forehead, and his eyes sparkled. "They shall have it," said he.

"Put yourself a bit straight," said John. Joe gave a pull at his necktie and a twitch at his jacket, and was off in a moment. Our master being one of the county magistrates, cases were often brought to him to settle, or say what should be done. In the stable we heard no more for some time, as it was the men's dinner hour, but when Joe came next into the stable I saw he was in high spirits; he gave me a good-natured slap, and said, "We won't see such things done, will we, old fellow?" We heard afterward that he had given his evidence so clearly, and the horses were in such an exhausted state, bearing marks of such brutal usage, that the carter was committed to take his trial, and might possibly be sentenced to two or three months in prison.

It was wonderful what a change had come over Joe. John laughed, and said he had grown an inch taller in that week, and I believe he had. He was just as kind and gentle as before, but there was more purpose and determination in all that he did—as if he had jumped at once from a boy into a man.

Nancy Springer lives in Pennsylvania with her family (and her horse). A gifted writer of adult fantasy novels, Nancy won the prestigious Nebula Award, given every year by the Science Fiction Writers of America, for her short story "The Boy Who Plaited Manes."

Recently, Nancy began writing for younger audiences. But whoever she is writing for, it's a good guess that you'll find horses at the center of the action—as in this humorous tale about a boy, a girl, and a horse named Suzie.

BARN GRAVITY

Nancy Springer

"Dare ya," Frog said.

We were walking home from school, the last day before summer vacation, me and Frog Lentz and Bad Ryan Stoner. Frog's real name is John, but everybody calls him Frog. My name is John, but everybody calls me John. I want them to call me something hot, like Flash or Ace.

But they just call me John.

Anyway, Bad Ryan was pushing, like always. He was saying I was a button-down nerd and a science-fair geek even if I didn't wear a pocket protector. Then he said he was going to have a girlfriend before the end of summer, and he wanted to bet me that I couldn't get one. And Frog was daring me to take the bet.

"Bet you ten bruisers," said Ryan.

Being punched in the arm even once by Bad Ryan Stoner was not anybody's idea of fun. I stood still in the middle of the sidewalk and thought. This was a serious bet.

"Dare ya!" Frog insisted. "Come on, John, there's gotta be *some* girl can like you!"

That was all there was to it, too. The girl had to say she liked me and she would go with me. We weren't old enough to date, so we didn't have to kiss or anything.

I flicked my hair back out of my eyes and tried to look cool. "Sure," I said to Bad Ryan. "You're on."

I knew what I was doing. Really. I had a secret weapon. I knew where half the girls in town would be all summer, and it was practically right behind my house.

Mrs. Lynchmont's boarding stable and riding school.

One thing I had noticed about girls, they're almost all crazy about horses. Personally, I could never understand how anybody could like a horse that much. They're all the same. Cloppy feet, long nose, swishy tail. Big deal. But girls think they're wonderful. Lucky for me. I could pretend to think they were wonderful, too.

Next morning I started. This bet of Ryan's wasn't something I could afford to put off till later.

I brushed my teeth and everything, then rode my bike down the hill behind my house to hang around at the stable like the other horse-lovers.

It was just as I thought it would be. All the foxiest girls in school were there, in tall black boots and skinny riding pants, looking just—wow. There were some chunky, plain-faced girls too, but I didn't pay any attention to them. And there were a lot of horses being patted or brushed or saddled, but I didn't pay any attention to them either. Right away I picked out the two girls who impressed me most: Karleigh Reynolds and Jade Ames. They had their hair smoothed back under their black velveteen riding hats, and their eyes shadowed by the brims, and they looked *mean.* They knew me from school, too, and I tried to look cool when they turned around and stared at me. It was hard, because every other girl in the place was staring at me, too.

So I was the only boy there. So what?

So I got back on my bike and got the heck out of there, that was what.

But I came back to the stable in the afternoon. Felt as if I'd better give my plan another try. It was getting hot, so most of the horseback riders had gone home. But Jade and Karleigh were still there, messing around with sponges and brushes and bridles and water buckets. They stared at me again when I rode in on my bike. The horses behind the fences lifted their long heads and stared at me, too. And nobody said hi.

"What are *you* doing here?" Karleigh complained.

I acted as if I hadn't heard her. "Yo, Jade. Hi, Karleigh," I said in my coolest voice while I parked my bike and walked over to them. "Whatcha doing?"

"We're robbing a bank," Jade said sarcastically. Okay, so anybody could see she was cleaning the bits on the bridles, but that was no reason for her to act so stuck-up. She didn't even *pretend* to smile. "What do you want?" she grumped at me.

I shrugged. "I like to hang around the horses."

"Sure."

"I do! I really like horses." To change the subject, I picked up one of the buckets that had a little soapy water in the bottom and swung it up over my head. The girls yelled at me and jumped up, but the water didn't slop out. I felt good that my experiment was working. Science was a subject I knew something about. More than I did about horses. "You know why the water stays in?" I asked, keeping the bucket going in a big circle.

"Who cares!" yelled Jade.

"You jerk, cut it out!"

85

Karleigh sounded as though she meant business, so I set the bucket down, but I kept talking. "Most people say it's because of centrifugal force, but there's no such thing as centrifugal force. The actual effect is caused by a combination of inertia and centripetal force overcoming the force of gravity."

Karleigh said, "Most people say people who swing things around in stables are asking to be killed."

"By what?"

"By a spooked horse, Einstein."

If she was giving me a nickname, it wasn't the kind I wanted. I wished she'd just call me John.

"You like horses, do you?" Jade put in. She and Karleigh were standing there looking at me, and there was this yellow horse standing beside them with its head over the fence looking at me too, and they all had the same expression. Suspicious, sort of Like they didn't believe me. It made me a little mad.

"Sure, I love horses," I said, edging away from the yellow one.

"I bet you ride, too," said Jade.

"Sure!"

"You ever had lessons?"

"What would I need lessons for? Riding is easy." I had never been on a horse, but there couldn't be much to it. Just get on the horse and make it go and steer by the reins. I knew exactly how I'd do it. "Getting from one place to another is just a physics problem," I explained. "Whether you do it on a horse or a rocket. Impulsion. Vectors. All it requires is an understanding of the principles of science."

Jade looked at Karleigh and Karleigh looked at Jade and they grinned cat grins at each other. Then Karleigh said, "Right. Fine. So let's go for a ride."

Even though I was making a good progress toward getting a

girlfriend, all of a sudden I wasn't happy. "Uh," I said, "I don't have a horse."

"No problem!" Jade turned and patted the long yellow head by her side. "Meet Suzie."

I swallowed and nodded at Suzie. Suzie stomped a fly off one big hoof and blinked at me with huge dark blue-brown eyes, and I knew right then my life was out of control.

It turned out Suzie was a horse any rider who boarded at the stable could borrow for a friend. I guess that made me a friend, sort of. Anyway, within a couple of minutes Karleigh and Jade had Suzie in the barn and saddled and bridled and out of the barn, waiting for me to ride her. Those two girls didn't mess around. Next they were putting one of those black velvety hard hats on me, buckling the harness under my chin. I had a feeling it didn't look half as cute on me as it would on one of them.

"I don't need to wear this," I said.

"Rules," Jade told me, but she was giggling. They were both giggling.

"Aw, come on!"

"It's to keep you from busting your Einstein head and spilling your Einstein brains," Karleigh said. "Get on the horse."

"What about you guys?"

"Just get on, John."

Karleigh had a way about her that made a person do what she said. I got on Suzie. It took a couple of tries, but when Jade came toward me to give me a boost, all of a sudden I managed. I didn't want Jade pushing my butt up into the saddle.

Suzie wasn't a tall horse, but she was round. She felt big as a sofa under me. I couldn't get my legs around her the way I thought I would. When I looked down between her fuzzy yellow ears, the ground seemed awfully far away.

Karleigh was holding Suzie's bridle for me. That should have told me something.

Jade pointed toward the riding ring gate. "Take her over there and ride around," she told me. "Don't try to go any faster than a walk."

"Sure," I said. Sounded good to me.

"All yours," said Karleigh, and she let go of the bridle.

I started to gather up my reins to turn Suzie toward the ring. But she gave a jerk of her head, pulled the reins right out of my hands, and jumped into a fast trot, going in the other direction. I yelled and grabbed at her mane, because she was bouncing me around on top of the saddle and I had already lost my stirrups. I could hear Jade and Karleigh laughing, but the sound echoed in a sort of tunnel. I ducked my head. Quick as a hungry dog going for supper, Suzie had trotted me into the barn, into the dark aisle. She made a hard right into one of the stalls, switched around in a tight circle, then stopped where she was with a grunt. I didn't know horses could grunt. Suzie sounded like a pig settling into its own personal mud after a good meal. "There," the grunt said, "I'm content."

I straightened up and let go of Suzie's mane—it was almost white and kind of short and stood up in soft spikes. I patted at her mane with my hands, trying to get it to lie down. It felt warm and coarse and wouldn't do anything I wanted it to. I decided that Suzie was not going to respond to the principles of physics and started to get down off her, but Karleigh came to the stall door. "Stay on her," she said, and she took her by the bridle and led her out of the stall. "Suzie," the tag on the stall door said. I could hear Jade having hysterics outside somewhere, but Karleigh was just grinning.

She led Suzie into the riding ring and closed the gate behind her before she let go of the bridle. "Okay," she said, "now you can ride her." She ducked outside the fence to watch, and Jade came and stood beside her. Jade had sort of

stopped laughing, but I had a feeling she was expecting to start again.

Which she did. Real soon. Because when I tried to get Suzie moving, all she did was ooze over against the gate we had just come in. She stood stuck against it like a big blob of yellow taffy, and I couldn't get her moving for anything.

"Kick her," said Karleigh.

"I am kicking!" I yelled. At least I was with the foot that was not squished against the gate. I was getting mad from being laughed at, and I gave Suzie a real good kick. She jumped into that fat-dog trot of hers, and I tried to slow her down to a walk, but all she did was turn a tight circle and come back and press against the gate again, so hard her yellow fur poked through to the other side.

I had had enough. "What is the *matter* with this horse!" I hollered.

"Barn gravity," Karleigh said. "It's the universal force of attraction between horses and their barns. It actually rearranges the molecular structure of the horse. See? Look at Suzie. Her molecules are leaking through the fence toward the barn."

Karleigh kept her face straight, but Jade laid her head down on the fence and howled.

"Sure," I said, grumpy. I know when I'm being made fun of. "So would you please unleak her so I can get down? Thanks for putting me on a horse nobody can ride."

Karleigh looked at me with a really strange smile. Then she ducked through the fence into the ring, took Suzie by the bridle, and led her away from the gate. I got off and turned to leave. When I turned back to see if Karleigh was following, she was on Suzie, riding her around the ring.

I was so surprised I hollered, "Hey! How come she's not leaking toward the barn anymore?"

"Application of scientific principles," Karleigh sang back.

That did it. I knew I had to learn how to overcome Suzie's

barn gravity if I was ever going to face the kids in school again, after what Karleigh and Jade would tell them.

"Okay, okay!" I yelled back. "So you can ride the horse, and I can't. I can't ride worth a darn, right?"

"Right!" agreed Jade from the fence.

"So will you guys show me how?" As soon as I said it, I realized I was smarter than I looked. All of a sudden I had a reason for hanging around Jade and Karleigh. I had a better chance of getting one of them to go with me.

Karleigh stopped Suzie. Karleigh and Jade quit grinning and giggling. They stared at me curiously. Suzie stared at me, too. I took off that stupid black velveteen hat, scratched my head where my hair was matted down, gave up on looking cool, and stared back at all three of them.

"How come?" Karleigh wanted to know.

"Why not?" I said, and that seemed to settle it.

They started by taking Suzie back to her stall and teaching me how to rub her down. She grunted at me.

Every afternoon for the next couple of weeks I went down to the stable. By the end of the second week, Suzie had stepped on my feet six times. She had knocked me over twice with her big, bony nose. She had left slobbery green horse kisses on fourteen of my T-shirts. She had puffed horse breath in my ear and chewed my hair. And I was riding her around the ring.

With Jade and Karleigh I wasn't getting that far. They had stopped laughing at me. In fact, they seemed bored with me.

"Every time I try to ride Suzie in a circle, it turns into an egg-shape pointing toward the barn," I told Karleigh. "Every time I ride her in a straight line past the barn, the line bends. It's amazing! That barn gravity warps geometric figures and everything."

"Right, John." Now that it was no longer just her joke, Karleigh was tired of it. But the whole idea fascinated me.

"It really does rearrange Suzie's molecular structure. It

bends her whole body. She bulges toward the barn. To keep her going, you got to kick her in the bulge."

"Right, John."

I kept working with Suzie. I got so I could trot and canter on her as well as walk. Sometimes I went down to ride her in the evenings. Mrs. Lynchmont didn't mind. She said nobody had ever paid so much attention to Suzie before. Everybody went for the big, tall Thoroughbred horses.

Sometimes I just went down to bring Suzie a treat, a carrot, a few jellybeans, so she wouldn't think all she was good for was to ride. She got so she would come over to the fence when she saw me, and I would rub her head and smooth down her forelock between those big blue-brown eyes of hers and say nice things to her. "Good fat-face," I'd tell her. "Nice flea brain. Good old airhead."

Suzie started to understand what I wanted when I rode her. When she did the right thing, I would pat her, and she would arch her creamy yellow neck and look proud. Pretty soon I would be able to ride her out on the trail. With Jade and Karleigh, maybe. But they didn't seem the least bit excited when I told them.

One day I was riding Suzie in the ring, trying to trot her in circles that weren't shaped like eggs with the pointy end toward the barn, when I saw Frog Lentz and Bad Ryan Stoner ride in on their bikes. I saw Jade and Karleigh walk up to them to say hi, and just by the way those girls walked I knew.

Frog and Ryan had found themselves girlfriends.

The four of them talked for a long time. I just kept riding Suzie. Afterward, after I had rubbed Suzie down and brushed her dry and checked her legs and feet, and I was just sort of standing around playing with her mane, I asked Jade, "Where'd you two meet those guys, anyway?"

"Huh?" She goggled at me. "At the Rollerway, Einstein!

Everybody knows the coolest guys hang out at the skating rink." Then her ride came, and she and Karleigh went home.

I leaned against Suzie's big yellow belly, thinking about my bet with Bad Ryan. I hadn't really done much about getting a girlfriend for a while. I guessed I could start over, start coming to the stable in the mornings again. There were plenty of girls who came there besides Jade and Karleigh. I had even talked to a few of them. Some of them were almost as cute as Suzie.

She swung her long head toward me, and I rubbed the soft fur around her ears. Yellow wasn't really a pretty enough name for the color she was. It was more of a creamy gold, like spun honey. Her mane and tail were even lighter, sort of a sunny white. She had a wide, gentle forehead with a white star on it, right between those big, soft eyes of hers. And eyelashes—she had enough blinky, sleepy eyelashes for six mascara ads.

I stood at the stall door, looked up and down the stable aisle to make sure nobody was around, took Suzie's head between my hands, and gave her a big, sloppy human kiss on her long face.

Sure, I could start making friends with some of the other girls at the stable. Not just the long-legged Thoroughbreds like Jade and Karleigh. Some of the chunky, plain-faced ones. Suzie had taught me not to always go for the Thoroughbreds.

But if that didn't work—what the heck, ten bruisers wasn't going to be so bad.

Or maybe Ryan Stoner would move away. Or maybe I could just tell him the truth. "Sure thing," I would say to him, real cool. "I've got a girlfriend who's nuts about me. You should see her. She's kind of a ditz-brain. But she has this soft, golden hair—and the biggest blue-brown eyes you've ever seen."

Award-winning poet Ruth Stone says she is "obsessed by poetry and language." That's easy to believe. She published her first poem (in the New York Times*) when she was still in grade school and hasn't stopped writing since. She was born in Virginia, grew up in Indiana, and now lives in Vermont. She has six grandchildren.*

ORCHARD

The mare roamed soft about the slope,
Her rump was like a dancing girl's.
Gentle beneath the apple trees
She pulled the grass and shook the flies.
Her forelocks hung in tawny curls;
She had a woman's limpid eyes,
A woman's patient stare that grieves.

And when she moved among the trees,
The dappled trees, her look was shy,
She hid her nakedness in leaves.
A delicate though weighted dance
She stepped while flocks of finches flew
From tree to tree and shot the leaves
With songs of golden twittering;
How admirable her tender stance.
And then the apple trees were new,
And she was new, and we were new,
And in the barns the stallions stamped
And shook the hills with trumpeting.

—Ruth Stone

Nathaniel Hawthorne, who was born in 1804, is often thought of as a rather gloomy writer. And indeed, his most well-known book, The Scarlet Letter, *is a novel of deep tragedy. But we can see another side of the great writer in his lyrical retellings of great Greek myths, which are collected in a volume called* Tanglewood Tales.

Here he tells the story of Pegasus. Today many people mistakenly call any horse with wings a Pegasus. But that is no more correct than calling all dogs Rex. Pegasus is the name of a specific winged horse. His story has been told many times—but rarely with such vivid and exciting details as those created here by Nathaniel Hawthorne.

THE

WINGED HORSE

Nathaniel Hawthorne

Once, in the old, old times a fountain gushed out of a hillside in the marvellous land of Greece. And for aught I know, after so many thousand years, it is still gushing out of the very self-same spot. At any rate, there was the pleasant fountain sparkling down the hillside in the golden sunset, when a handsome young man named Bellerophon drew near its margin. In his hand he held a magic bridle, studded with brilliant gems, and adorned with a golden bit.

Seeing an old man, and another of middle age, and a little

boy, near the fountain, and likewise a maiden, he paused, and begged that he might refresh himself.

"This is very delicious water," he said to the maiden, as he rinsed and filled her pitcher. "Will you be kind enough to tell me whether the fountain has any name?"

"Yes; it is called the Fountain of Pirene," answered the maiden.

"This, then, is Pirene? I thank you for telling me its name. I have come from a faraway country to find this very spot."

A middle-aged country fellow stared hard at young Bellerophon, and at the handsome bridle which he carried in his hand.

"The watercourses must be getting low, friend, in your part of the world," remarked he, "if you come so far only to find the Fountain of Pirene. Pray, have you lost a horse? I see you carry the bridle in your hand; and a very pretty one it is, with that double row of bright stones upon it."

"I have lost no horse," said Bellerophon, with a smile. "But I happen to be seeking a very famous one, which, as wise people have informed me, must be found hereabouts. Do you know whether the winged horse Pegasus still haunts the Fountain of Pirene, as he used to do in your forefathers' days?"

The country fellow laughed.

"Pegasus, indeed!" cried he, turning up his nose as high as such a flat nose could be turned up. "Pegasus, indeed! A winged horse, truly! Why, friend, are you in your senses? Of what use would wings be to a horse? I don't believe in Pegasus. There never was such a ridiculous kind of a horse-fowl made!"

"I have reason to think otherwise," said Bellerophon.

And then he turned to an old, gray man, who was leaning on a staff, and listening very attentively, with his head stretched forward, and one hand at his ear.

"And what say you, venerable sir?" inquired he. "In your

younger days, I should imagine, you must frequently have seen the winged steed!"

"Ah, young stranger, my memory is very poor!" said the aged man. "When I was a lad, if I remember rightly, I used to believe there was such a horse, and so did everybody else."

"And have you never seen him, my fair maiden?" asked Bellerophon of the girl.

"Once I thought I saw him," replied the maiden, with a smile and a blush. "It was either Pegasus or a large white bird, a very great way up in the air. And one other time, as I was coming to the fountain with my pitcher, I heard a neigh. Oh, such a brisk and melodious neigh as that was! My heart leaped with delight at the sound. But it startled me, nevertheless; so that I ran home without filling my pitcher."

"That was truly a pity!" said Bellerophon.

And he turned to the child, who was gazing up at him with his rosy mouth wide open.

"Well, my little fellow," cried Bellerophon, playfully pulling one of his curls, "I suppose you have often seen the winged horse."

"That I have," answered the child, very readily. "I saw him yesterday, and many times before."

"You are a fine little man!" said Bellerophon, drawing the child closer to him. "Come, tell me all about it."

"Why," replied the child, "I often come here to sail little boats in the fountain. And sometimes, when I look down into the water, I see the image of the winged horse in the picture of the sky that is there."

And Bellerophon put his faith in the child, who had seen the image of Pegasus in the water, and in the maiden, who had heard him neigh so melodiously.

Therefore, he hunted about the Fountain of Pirene for a great many days afterward.

Now you will, perhaps, wish to be told why it was that Bellerophon had undertaken to catch the winged horse. It will be quite enough to say that in a certain country of Asia, a terrible monster, called a Chimera, had made its appearance. This Chimera was nearly, if not quite, the ugliest and most poisonous creature, and the strangest and unaccountablest, and the hardest to fight with, and the most difficult to run away from, that ever came out of the earth's inside. It had a tail like a boa constrictor; its body was like I do not care what; and it had three separate heads, one of which was a lion's, the second a goat's, and the third an abominably great snake's. And a hot blast of fire came flaming out of each of its three mouths!

With its flaming breath, it could set a forest on fire, or burn up a field of grain, or, for that matter, a village, with all its fences and houses. It laid waste the whole country round about.

While the hateful beast was doing all these horrible things, it so chanced that Bellerophon came to that part of the world on a visit to the King. The King's name was Iobates, and Lycia was the country which he ruled over. Bellerophon was one of the bravest youths in the world, and desired nothing so much as to do some valiant deed, such as would make all mankind admire and love him. In those days, the only way for a young man to distinguish himself was by fighting battles, either with the enemies of his country or with wicked giants, or with troublesome dragons, or with wild beasts, when he could find nothing more dangerous to encounter. King Iobates, perceiving the courage of his youthful visitor, proposed to him to go and fight the Chimera, which everybody was afraid of, and which, unless it should be soon killed, was likely to convert Lycia into a desert. Bellerophon hesitated not a moment, but assured the King that he would either slay this Chimera or perish in the attempt.

But in the first place, as the monster was so prodigiously swift, he bethought himself that he should never win the victory by fighting on foot. The wisest thing he could do, therefore, was to get the very best and fleetest horse that could anywhere be found. And what other horse in all the world was half so fleet as the marvellous horse Pegasus, who had wings as well as legs, and was even more active in the air than on the earth? To be sure, a great many people denied that there was any such horse with wings.

Well was it for Bellerophon that the child had grown so fond of him, and was never weary of keeping him company. Every morning the child gave him a new hope.

"Dear Bellerophon," he would cry, looking up hopefully into his face, "I think we shall see Pegasus today!"

And at length, if it had not been for the little boy's unwavering faith, Bellerophon would have given up all hope, and would have gone back to Lycia and have done his best to slay the Chimera without the help of the winged horse.

One morning the child spoke to Bellerophon even more hopefully than usual.

"Dear, dear Bellerophon," cried he, "I know not why it is, but I feel as if we should certainly see Pegasus today!"

And all that day he would not stir a step from Bellerophon's side. So they ate a crust of bread together, and drank some of the water of the fountain. In the afternoon there they sat, and, when he least thought of it, Bellerophon felt the pressure of the child's little hand, and heard a soft, almost breathless whisper.

"See there, dear Bellerophon! There is an image in the water!"

The young man looked down into the fountain, and saw what he took to be the reflection of a bird which seemed to be flying at a great height in the air, with a gleam of sunshine on its snowy wings.

"What a splendid bird it must be!" said he. "And how very large it looks, though it must really be flying higher than the clouds!"

"It makes me tremble!" whispered the child. "I am afraid

to look up into the air! Dear Bellerophon, do you not see that it is no bird? It is the winged horse Pegasus!"

Bellerophon's heart began to throb! He caught the child in his arms, and shrank back with him, so that they were both hidden among the thick shrubbery which grew all around the fountain.

Nearer and nearer came the aerial wonder. Downward came Pegasus, in wide, sweeping circles, which grew narrower and narrower still as he approached the earth. At last, with so slight a pressure as hardly to bend the grass about the fountain, he alighted, and, stooping his wild head, began to drink.

After drinking to his heart's content, the winged horse began to caper to and fro and dance, as it were out of mere idleness and sport.

At length, Pegasus folded his wings, and lay down on the soft green turf. But being too full of aerial life to remain quiet for many moments together, he soon rolled over on his back, with his four slender legs in the air.

Finally, when he had had enough of rolling over and over, Pegasus turned himself about, and, indolently, like any other horse, put out his forelegs, in order to rise from the ground; and Bellerophon, who had guessed that he would do so, darted suddenly from the thicket, and leaped astride of his back.

Yes, there he sat, on the back of the winged horse!

But what a bound did Pegasus make, when, for the first time, he felt the weight of a mortal man upon his loins! Before he had time to draw a breath, Bellerophon found himself five hundred feet aloft, and still shooting upward, while the winged horse snorted and trembled with terror and anger. Upward he went, up, up, up, until he plunged into the cold misty bosom of a cloud.

He skimmed straight forward, and sideways, and backward. He reared himself erect, with his forelegs on a wreath of mist, and his hind legs on nothing at all. He flung out his heels behind, and put down his head between his legs, with his wings pointing right upward. At about two miles' height above the earth, he turned a somersault, so that Bellerophon's heels were where his head should have been, and he seemed to look down into the sky, instead of up. He twisted his head about, and looking Bellerophon in the face, with fire flashing from his eyes, made a terrible attempt to bite him. He fluttered his pinions so wildly that one of the silver feathers was shaken out, and floating earthward, was picked up by the child, who kept it as long as he lived, in memory of Pegasus and Bellerophon.

But the latter (who, as you may judge, was as good a horseman as ever galloped) had been watching his opportunity, and at last clapped the golden bit of the enchanted bridle between the winged steed's jaws. No sooner was this done than Pegasus became as manageable as if he had taken food all his life out of Bellerophon's hand.

While Pegasus had been doing his utmost to shake Bellerophon off his back, he had flown a very long distance; and they had come within sight of a lofty mountain by the time the bit was in his mouth. Bellerophon had seen this mountain before, and knew it to be Helicon, on the summit of which was the winged horse's abode. Thither Pegasus now flew, and, alighting, waited patiently until Bellerophon should please to dismount. The young man, accordingly, leaped from the steed's back, but still held him fast by the bridle. Meeting his eyes, however, he was so affected by the thought of the free life which Pegasus had heretofore lived, that he could not bear to keep him a prisoner if he really desired his liberty.

Obeying this generous impulse, he slipped the enchanted bridle off the head of Pegasus.

"Leave me, Pegasus!" said he. "Either leave me, or love me."

In an instant, the winged horse shot almost out of sight,

soaring straight upward from the summit of Mount Helicon. Ascending higher and higher, he looked like a bright speck, and at last could no longer be seen in the hollow waste of the sky. And Bellerophon was afraid that he should never behold him more. But while he was lamenting his own folly, the bright speck reappeared, and drew nearer and nearer, until it descended lower than the sunshine; and behold, Pegasus had come back! After this, there was no more fear of the winged horse making his escape. He and Bellerophon were friends, and put loving faith in one another.

That night they lay down and slept together, with Bellerophon's arm about the neck of Pegasus.

In this manner, Bellerophon and the wondrous steed spent several days, and grew better acquainted and fonder of each other all the time. They went on long journeys, and sometimes ascended so high that the earth looked hardly bigger than—the moon. They visited distant countries, and amazed the inhabitants. A thousand miles a day was no more than an easy space for the fleet Pegasus to pass over. Bellerophon was delighted with this kind of life, and would have liked nothing better than to live always in the same way, but he could not forget the horrible Chimera, which he had promised King Iobates to slay. So, at last, when he had become well accustomed to feats of horsemanship in the air, and could manage Pegasus with the least motion of his hand, and had taught him to obey his voice, he determined to attempt the performance of this perilous adventure.

He then turned the head of Pegasus toward the east, and set out for Lycia. In their flight they overtook an eagle, and came so nigh him, before he could get out of their way, that Bellerophon might easily have caught him by the leg. Hastening onward at this rate, it was still early in the forenoon when they beheld the lofty mountains of Lycia.

There was nothing remarkable to be detected, at first sight, in any of the valleys and dells that lay among the

precipitous heights of the mountains. Nothing at all; unless, indeed, it were three spires of black smoke, which issued from what seemed to be the mouth of a cavern, and clambered sullenly into the atmosphere.

Bellerophon made a sign, which the winged horse understood, and sunk slowly through the air, until his hoofs were scarcely more than a man's height above the rocky bottom of the valley. In front, as far off as you could throw a stone, was the cavern's mouth.

There seemed to be a heap of strange and terrible creatures curled up within the cavern. Their bodies lay so close together that Bellerophon could not distinguish them apart; but, judging by their heads, one of these creatures was a huge snake, the second a fierce lion, and the third an ugly goat. The lion and the goat were asleep; the snake was broad awake, and kept staring about him with a great pair of fiery eyes. But—and this was the most wonderful part of the matter—the three spires of smoke evidently issued from the nostrils of these three heads! So strange was the spectacle that, though Bellerophon had been expecting it, the truth did not immediately occur to him that here was the terrible three-headed Chimera.

Pegasus sent forth a neigh that sounded like the call of a trumpet to battle. At this sound the three heads reared themselves erect, and belched out great flashes of flame. Before Bellerophon had time to consider what to do next, the monster flung itself out of the cavern and sprung straight towards him, with its immense claws extended, and its snaky tail twisting itself venomously behind. If Pegasus had not been as nimble as a bird, both he and his rider would have been overthrown by the Chimera's headlong rush, and thus the battle have been ended before it was well begun. But the winged horse was not to be caught so. In the twinkling of an eye he was up aloft, halfway to the clouds, snorting with anger.

The Chimera, on the other hand, raised itself up so as to stand absolutely on the tip end of its tail, with its talons pawing fiercely in the air, and its three heads spluttering fire at Pegasus and his rider. Bellerophon, meanwhile, was fitting his shield on his arm, and drawing his sword.

"Now, my beloved Pegasus," he whispered in the winged horse's ear, "thou must help me to slay this insufferable monster; or else thou shalt fly back to thy solitary mountain peak without thy friend Bellerophon."

Pegasus whinnied, and, turning back his head, rubbed his nose tenderly against his rider's cheek.

"I thank you, Pegasus," answered Bellerophon. "Now, then, let us make a dash at the monster!"

Uttering these words, he shook the bridle; and Pegasus darted down aslant, as swift as the flight of an arrow; right toward the Chimera's threefold head, which all this time was poking itself as high as it could into the air. As he came within arm's length, Bellerophon made a cut at the monster, but was carried onward by his steed before he could see whether the blow had been successful.

Pegasus continued his course, but soon wheeled round, at about the same distance from the Chimera as before. Bellerophon then perceived that he had cut the goat's head of the monster almost off, so that it dangled downward by the skin, and seemed quite dead.

But, to make amends, the snake's head and the lion's head had taken all the fierceness of the dead one into themselves, and spit flame, and hissed, and roared, with a vast deal more fury than before.

"Never mind, my brave Pegasus!" cried Bellerophon. "With another stroke like that, we will stop either its hissing or its roaring."

And again he shook the bridle. Dashing aslantwise as before, the winged horse made another arrow flight toward the Chimera, and Bellerophon aimed another downright stroke

at one of the two remaining heads as he shot by. But this time neither he nor Pegasus escaped so well as at first. With one of its claws the Chimera had given the young man a deep scratch on his shoulder, and had slightly damaged the left wing of the flying steed with the other. On his part Bellerophon had mortally wounded the lion's head of the monster, insomuch that it now hung downward, with its fire almost extinguished, and sending out gasps of thick black smoke.

"Dost thou bleed, my immortal horse?" cried the young man, caring less for his own hurt than for the anguish of this glorious creature, that ought never to have tasted pain. "The execrable Chimera shall pay for this mischief with his last head!"

Then he shook the bridle, shouted loudly, and guided Pegasus not slantwise as before, but straight at the monster's hideous front. So rapid was the onset, that it seemed but a dazzle and a flash before Bellerophon was at close grips with his enemy.

The Chimera, by this time, after losing its second head, had got into a red-hot passion of pain and rampant rage. It so flounced about, half on earth and partly in the air, that it was impossible to say which element it rested upon. It opened its snake jaws to such an abominable width that Pegasus might almost have flown right down its throat, wings outspread, rider and all! At their approach it shot out a tremendous blast of its fiery breath, and enveloped Bellerophon and his steed in a perfect atmosphere of flame, singeing the wings of Pegasus, scorching off one whole side of the young man's golden ringlets.

But this was nothing to what followed.

When the airy rush of the winged horse had brought him within the distance of a hundred yards, the Chimera gave a spring, and flung its huge, awkward, venomous, and utterly detestable carcass right upon poor Pegasus, clung round him with might and main, and tied up his snaky tail into a knot!

Up flew the aerial steed, higher, higher, higher, above the mountain peaks, above the clouds, and almost out of sight of the solid earth. But still the earthborn monster kept its hold, and was borne upward, along with the creature of light and air.

Bellerophon, meanwhile, turning about, found himself face to face with the ugly grimness of the Chimera's visage, and could only avoid being scorched to death, or bitten right in twain, by holding up his shield. Over the upper edge of the shield he looked sternly into the savage eyes of the monster.

But the Chimera was so mad and wild with pain, that it did not guard itself well. In its efforts to stick its horrible iron claws into its enemy, the creature left its own breast exposed; and perceiving this, Bellerophon thrust his sword up to the hilt into its cruel heart. Immediately the snaky tail untied its knot. The monster let go its hold of Pegasus, and fell from that vast height, downward. The fire within its bosom, instead of being put out, burned fiercer than ever, and quickly began to consume the dead carcass.

Thus it fell out of the sky, all aflame, and (it being nightfall before it reached the earth) was mistaken for a shooting star or a comet. But, at early sunrise, some cottagers were going to their day's labor, and saw, to their astonishment, that several acres of ground were strewn with black ashes. In the middle of a field there was a heap of whitened bones a great deal higher than a haystack. Nothing else was ever seen of the dreadful Chimera!

And when Bellerophon had won the victory, he bent forward and kissed Pegasus, while the tears stood in his eyes.

$\mathcal{M}$ary O'Hara was a successful screenwriter who left Hollywood to live with her husband on a Wyoming ranch, where she hoped to concentrate on writing music. And indeed, she published a number of musical compositions. But as she herself said, "I was destined to be a writer." When "My Friend Flicka" was published in Story magazine, her editor urged her to turn it into a novel. She followed his advice, and the book became enormously popular. The book was turned into a motion picture and later a television show.

But the beautiful short story that follows is what started it all.

$\mathcal{M}$Y $\mathcal{F}$RIEND $\mathcal{F}$LICKA

Mary O'Hara

Report cards for the second semester were sent out soon after school closed in mid-June.

Kennie's was a shock to the whole family.

"If I could have a colt all for my own," said Kennie, "I might do better."

Rob McLaughlin glared at his son. "Just as a matter of curiosity," he said, "how do you go about it to get a *zero* in an examination? Forty in arithmetic; seventeen in history! But a *zero?* Just as one man to another, what goes on in your head?"

"Yes, tell us how you do it, Ken," chirped Howard.

"Eat your breakfast, Howard," snapped his mother.

Kennie's blond head bent over his plate until his face was almost hidden. His cheeks burned.

McLaughlin finished his coffee and pushed his chair back. "You'll do an hour a day on your lessons all through the summer."

Nell McLaughlin saw Kennie wince as if something had actually hurt him.

Lessons and study in the summertime, when the long winter was just over and there weren't hours enough in the day for all the things he wanted to do!

Kennie took things hard. His eyes turned to the wide open window with a look almost of despair.

The hill opposite the house, covered with arrow-straight jack pines, was sharply etched in the thin air of the eight-thousand-foot altitude. Where it fell away, vivid green grass ran up to meet it; and over range and upland poured the strong Wyoming sunlight that stung everything into burning color. A big jack rabbit sat under one of the pines, waving his long ears back and forth.

Ken had to look at his plate and blink back tears before he could turn to his father and say carelessly, "Can I help you in the corral with the horses this morning, Dad?"

"You'll do your study every morning before you do anything else." And McLaughlin's scarred boots and heavy spurs clattered across the kitchen floor. "I'm disgusted with you. Come, Howard."

Howard strode after his father, nobly refraining from looking at Kennie.

"Help me with the dishes, Kennie," said Nell McLaughlin as she rose, tied on a big apron, and began to clear the table.

Kennie looked at her in despair. She poured steaming water into the dishpan and sent him for the soap powder.

"If I could have a colt," he muttered again.

"Now get busy with that dish towel, Ken. It's eight o'clock. You can study till nine and then go up to the corral. They'll still be there."

At supper that night Kennie said, "But Dad, Howard had a

colt all of his own when he was only eight. And he trained it and schooled it all himself; and now he's eleven, and Highboy is three, and he's riding him. I'm nine now, and even if you did give me a colt now I couldn't catch up to Howard because I couldn't ride it till it was a three-year-old, and then I'd be twelve."

Nell laughed. "Nothing wrong with that arithmetic."

But Rob said, "Howard never gets less than a seventy-five average at school, and hasn't disgraced himself and his family by getting more demerits than any other boy in his class."

Kennie didn't answer. He couldn't figure it out. He tried hard; he spent hours poring over his books. That was supposed to get you good marks, but it never did. Everyone said he was bright. Why was it that when he studied he didn't learn? He had a vague feeling that perhaps he looked out the window too much, or looked through the walls to see clouds and sky and hills and wonder what was happening out there. Sometimes it wasn't even a wonder, but just a pleasant drifting feeling of nothing at all, as if nothing mattered, as if there was always plenty of time, as if the lessons would get done of themselves. And then the bell would ring, and study period was over.

If he had a colt . . .

When the boys had gone to bed that night Nell McLaughlin sat down with her overflowing mending basket and glanced at her husband.

He was at his desk as usual, working on account books and inventories.

Nell threaded a darning needle and thought: It's either that whacking big bill from the vet for the mare that died or the last half of the tax bill.

It didn't seem just the auspicious moment to plead Kennie's cause. But then, these days, there was always a line between Rob's eyes and a harsh note in his voice.

"Rob," she began.

He flung down his pencil and turned around.

"Damn that law!" he exclaimed.

"What law?"

"The state law that puts high taxes on pedigreed stock. I'll have to do as the rest of 'em do—drop the papers."

"Drop the papers! But you'll never get decent prices if you don't have registered horses."

"I don't get decent prices now."

"But you will someday if you don't drop the papers."

"Maybe." He bent again over the desk.

Rob, thought Nell, was a lot like Kennie himself. He set his heart. Oh, how stubbornly he set his heart on just some one thing he wanted above everything else. He had set his heart on horses and ranching way back when he had been a crack rider at West Point; and he had resigned and thrown away his army career just for the horses. Well, he'd got what he wanted . . .

She drew a deep breath, snipped her thread, laid down the sock, and again looked across at her husband as she unrolled another length of darning cotton.

To get what you want is one thing, she was thinking. The three-thousand-acre ranch and the hundred head of horses. But to make it pay—for a dozen or more years they had been trying to make it pay. People said ranching hadn't paid since the beef barons ran their herds on public land; people said the only prosperous ranchers in Wyoming were the dude ranchers; people said . . .

But suddenly she gave her head a little rebellious, gallant shake. Rob would always be fighting and struggling against something, like Kennie, perhaps like herself, too. Even those first years when there was no water piped into the house, when every day brought a new difficulty or danger, how she had loved it! How she still loved it!

She ran the darning ball into the toe of a sock, Kennie's

sock. The length of it gave her a shock. Yes, the boys were growing up fast, and now Kennie—Kennie and the colt . . .

After a while she said, "Give Kennie a colt, Rob."

"He doesn't deserve it." The answer was short. Rob pushed away his papers and took out his pipe.

"Howard's too far ahead of him, older and bigger and quicker, and his wits about him, and—"

"Ken doesn't half try, doesn't stick at anything."

She put down her sewing. "He's crazy for a colt of his own. He hasn't had another idea in his head since you gave Highboy to Howard."

"I don't believe in bribing children to do their duty."

"Not a bribe." She hesitated.

"No? What would you call it?"

She tried to think it out. "I just have the feeling Ken isn't going to pull anything off, and"—her eyes sought Rob's—"it's time he did. It isn't the school marks alone, but I just don't want things to go on any longer with Ken never coming out at the right end of anything."

"I'm beginning to think he's just dumb."

"He's not dumb. Maybe a little thing like this—if he had a colt of his own, trained him, rode him—"

Rob interrupted. "But it isn't a little thing, nor an easy thing, to break and school a colt the way Howard has schooled Highboy. I'm not going to have a good horse spoiled by Ken's careless ways. He goes woolgathering. He never knows what he's doing."

"But he'd *love* a colt of his own, Rob. If he could do it, it might make a big difference in him."

"*If* he could do it! But that's a big if."

At breakfast the next morning Kennie's father said to him, "When you've done your study come out to the barn. I'm going in the car up to section twenty-one this morning to look over the brood mares. You can go with me."

"Can I go, too, Dad?" cried Howard.

McLaughlin frowned at Howard. "You turned Highboy out last evening with dirty legs."

Howard wriggled. "I groomed him—"

"Yes, down to his knees."

"He kicks."

"And whose fault is that? You don't get on his back again until I see his legs clean."

The two boys eyed each other, Kennie secretly triumphant and Howard chagrined. McLaughlin turned at the door, "And, Ken, a week from today I'll give you a colt. Between now and then you can decide what one you want."

Kennie shot out of his chair and stared at his father. "A—a spring colt, Dad, or a yearling?"

McLaughlin was somewhat taken aback, but his wife concealed a smile. If Kennie got a yearling colt, he would be even up with Howard.

"A yearling colt, your father means, Ken," she said smoothly. "Now hurry with your lessons. Howard will wipe."

Kennie found himself the most important personage on the ranch. Prestige lifted his head, gave him an inch more of height and a bold stare, and made him feel different all the way through. Even Gus and Tim Murphy, the ranch hands, were more interested in Kennie's choice of a colt than anything else.

Howard was fidgety with suspense. "Who'll you pick, Ken? Say—pick Doughboy, why don't you? Then when he grows up he'll be sort of twins with mine, in his name anyway. Doughboy, Highboy. See?"

The boys were sitting on the worn wooden step of the door which led from the tack room into the corral, busy with rags and polish, shining their bridles.

Ken looked at his brother with scorn. Doughboy would never have half of Highboy's speed.

"Lassie, then," suggested Howard. "She's black as ink, like mine. And she'll be fast—"

"Dad says Lassie'll never go over fifteen hands."

Nell McLaughlin saw the change in Kennie, and her hopes rose. He went to his books in the morning with determination and really studied. A new alertness took the place of the daydreaming. Examples in arithmetic were neatly written out, and as she passed his door before breakfast she often heard the monotonous drone of his voice as he read his American history aloud.

Each night, when he kissed her, he flung his arms around her and held her fiercely for a moment, then, with a winsome and blissful smile into her eyes, turned away to bed.

He spent days inspecting the different bands of horses and colts. He sat for hours on the corral fence, very important, chewing straws. He rode off on one of the ponies for half the day, wandering through the mile-square pastures that ran down toward the Colorado border.

And when the week was up he announced his decision. "I'll take that yearling filly of Rocket's. The sorrel with the cream tail and mane."

His father looked at him in surprise. "The one that got tangled in the barbed wire? That's never been named?"

In a second all Kennie's new pride was gone. He hung his head defensively. "Yes."

"You've made a bad choice, son. You couldn't have picked a worse."

"She's fast, Dad. And Rocket's fast—"

"It's the worst line of horses I've got. There's never one amongst them with real sense. The mares are hellions and the stallions outlaws; they're untamable."

"I'll tame her."

Rob guffawed. "Not I, nor anyone, has ever been able to really tame any one of them."

Kennie's chest heaved.

"Better change your mind, Ken. You want a horse that'll be a real friend to you, don't you?"

"Yes." Kennie's voice was unsteady.

"Well, you'll never make a friend of that filly. She's all cut and scarred up already with tearing through barbed wire after that bitch of a mother of hers. No fence'll hold 'em—"

"I know," said Kennie, still more faintly.

"Change your mind?" asked Howard briskly.

"No."

Rob was grim and put out. He couldn't go back on his word. The boy had to have a reasonable amount of help in breaking and taming the filly, and he could envision precious hours, whole days, wasted in the struggle.

Nell McLaughlin despaired. Once again Ken seemed to have taken the wrong turn and was back where he had begun—stoical, silent, defensive.

But there was a difference that only Ken could know. The way he felt about his colt. The way his heart sang. The pride and joy that filled him so full that sometimes he hung his head so they wouldn't see it shining out of his eyes.

He had known from the very first that he would choose that particular yearling because he was in love with her.

The year before, he had been out working with Gus, the big Swedish ranch hand, on the irrigation ditch, when they had noticed Rocket standing in a gully on the hillside, quiet for once, and eying them cautiously.

"Ay bet she got a colt," said Gus, and they walked carefully up the draw. Rocket gave a wild snort, thrust her feet out, shook her head wickedly, then fled away. And as they reached the spot they saw standing there the wavering, pinkish colt, barely able to keep its feet. It gave a little squeak and started after its mother on crooked, wobbling legs.

118

"Yee whiz! Luk at de little *flicka!*" said Gus.

"What does *flicka* mean, Gus?"

"Swedish for little gurl, Ken."

Ken announced at supper, "You said she'd never been named. I've named her. Her name is Flicka."

The first thing to do was to get her in. She was running with a band of yearlings on the saddleback, cut with ravines and gullies, on section twenty.

They all went out after her, Ken, as owner, on old Rob Roy, the wisest horse on the ranch.

Ken was entranced to watch Flicka when the wild band of youngsters discovered that they were being pursued and took off across the mountain. Footing made no difference to her. She floated across the ravines, always two lengths ahead of the others. Her pink mane and tail whipped in the wind. Her long delicate legs had only to aim, it seemed, at a particular spot, for her to reach it and sail on. She seemed to Ken a fairy horse.

He sat, motionless, just watching and holding Rob Roy in when his father thundered past on Sultan and shouted, "Well, what's the matter? Why didn't you turn 'em?"

Kennie woke up and galloped after.

Rob Roy brought in the whole band. The corral gates were closed, and an hour was spent shunting the ponies in and out and through the chutes, until Flicka was left alone in the small round corral in which the baby colts were branded. Gus drove the others away, out the gate, and up the saddleback.

But Flicka did not intend to be left. She hurled herself against the poles which walled the corral. She tried to jump them. They were seven feet high. She caught her front feet over the top rung, clung, scrambled, while Kennie held his breath for fear the slender legs would be caught between the bars and snapped. Her hold broke; she fell over backward, rolled, screamed, tore around the corral. Kennie had a sick

feeling in the pit of his stomach, and his father looked disgusted.

One of the bars broke. She hurled herself again. Another went. She saw the opening and, as neatly as a dog crawls through a fence, inserted her head and forefeet, scrambled through, and fled away, bleeding in a dozen places.

As Gus was coming back, just about to close the gate to the upper range, the sorrel whipped through it, sailed across the road and ditch with her inimitable floating leap, and went up the side of the saddleback like a jack rabbit.

From way up the mountain Gus heard excited whinnies, as she joined the band he had just driven up, and the last he saw of them they were strung out along the crest running like deer.

"Yee whiz!" said Gus, and stood motionless and staring until the ponies had disappeared over the ridge. Then he closed the gate, remounted Rob Roy, and rode back to the corral.

Rob McLaughlin gave Kennie one more chance to change his mind. "Last chance, son. Better pick a horse that you have some hope of riding one day. I'd have got rid of this whole line of stock if they weren't so damned fast that I've had the fool idea that someday there might turn out one gentle one in the lot—and I'd have a racehorse. But there's never been one so far, and it's not going to be Flicka."

"It's not going to be Flicka," chanted Howard.

"Perhaps she *might* be gentled," said Kennie; and Nell, watching, saw that although his lips quivered, there was fanatical determination in his eye.

"Ken," said Rob, "it's up to you. If you say you want her we'll get her. But she wouldn't be the first of that line to die rather than give in. They're beautiful and they're fast, but let me tell you this, young man, they're *loco!*"

Kennie flinched under his father's direct glance.

"If I go after her again I'll not give up whatever comes; understand what I mean by that?"

"Yes."

"What do you say?"

"I want her."

They brought her in again. They had better luck this time. She jumped over the Dutch half door of the stable and crashed inside. The men slammed the upper half of the door shut, and she was caught.

The rest of the band was driven away, and Kennie stood outside of the stable, listening to the wild hoofs beating, the screams, the crashes. His Flicka inside there! He was drenched with perspiration.

"We'll leave her to think it over," said Rob when dinnertime came. "Afterward we'll go up and feed and water her."

But when they went up afterward there was no Flicka in the barn. One of the windows, higher than the mangers, was broken.

The window opened onto a pasture an eighth of a mile square, fenced in barbed wire six feet high. Near the stable stood a wagonload of hay. When they went around the back of the stable to see where Flicka had hidden herself, they found her between the stable and the hay wagon, eating.

At their approach she leaped away, then headed east across the pasture.

"If she's like her mother," said Rob, "she'll go right through the wire."

"Ay bet she'll go over," said Gus. "She yumps like a deer."

"No horse can jump that," said McLaughlin.

Kennie said nothing because he could not speak. It was, perhaps, the most terrible moment of his life. He watched Flicka racing toward the eastern wire.

A few yards from it she swerved, turned, and raced diagonally south.

"It turned her! It turned her!" cried Kennie, almost sobbing. It was the first sign of hope for Flicka. "Oh, Dad! She has got sense. She has! She has!"

Flicka turned again as she met the southern boundary of the pasture, again at the northern; she avoided the barn. Without abating anything of her whirlwind speed, following a precise, accurate calculation and turning each time on a dime, she investigated every possibility. Then, seeing that there was no hope, she raced south toward the range where she had spent her life, gathered herself, and shot into the air.

Each of the three men watching had the impulse to cover his eyes, and Kennie gave a sort of a howl of despair.

Twenty yards of fence came down with her as she hurled herself through. Caught on the upper strands, she turned a complete somersault, landing on her back, her four legs dragging the wires down on top of her, and tangling herself in them beyond hope of escape.

"Damn the wire!" cursed McLaughlin. "If I could afford decent fences . . ."

Kennie followed the men miserably as they walked to the filly. They stood in a circle watching, while she kicked and fought and thrashed until the wire was tightly wound and knotted about her, cutting, piercing, and tearing great three-cornered pieces of flesh and hide. At last she was unconscious, streams of blood running on her golden coat, and pools of crimson widening and spreading on the grass beneath her.

With the wire cutter which Gus always carried in the hip pocket of his overalls he cut all the wire away, and they drew her into the pasture, repaired the fence, placed hay, a box of oats, and a tub of water near her, and called it a day.

"I don't think she'll pull out of it," said McLaughlin.

Next morning Kennie was up at five, doing his lessons. At six he went out to Flicka.

She had not moved. Food and water were untouched. She

124

was no longer bleeding, but the wounds were swollen and caked over.

Kennie got a bucket of fresh water and poured it over her mouth. Then he leaped away, for Flicka came to life, scrambled up, got her balance, and stood swaying.

Kennie went a few feet away and sat down to watch her. When he went in to breakfast, she had drunk deeply of the water and was mouthing the oats.

There began then a sort of recovery. She ate, drank, limped about the pasture, stood for hours with hanging head and weakly splayed-out legs, under the clump of cottonwood trees. The swollen wounds scabbed and began to heal.

Kennie lived in the pasture too. He followed her around; he talked to her. He, too, lay snoozing or sat under the cottonwoods; and often, coaxing her with hand outstretched, he walked very quietly toward her. But she would not let him come near her.

Often she stood with her head at the south fence, looking off to the mountain. It made the tears come to Kennie's eyes to see the way she longed to get away.

Still Rob said she wouldn't pull out of it. There was no use putting a halter on her. She had no strength.

One morning, as Ken came out of the house, Gus met him and said, "De filly's down."

Kennie ran to the pasture, Howard close behind him. The right hind leg which had been badly swollen at the knee joint had opened in a festering wound, and Flicka lay flat and motionless, with staring eyes.

"Don't you wish now you'd chosen Doughboy?" asked Howard.

"Go away!" shouted Ken.

Howard stood watching while Kennie sat down on the ground and took Flicka's head on his lap. Though she was conscious and moved a little, she did not struggle nor seem frightened. Tears rolled down Kennie's cheeks as he talked to her and petted her. After a few moments Howard walked away.

"Mother, what do you do for an infection when it's a horse?" asked Kennie.

"Just what you'd do if it was a person. Wet dressing. I'll help you, Ken. We mustn't let those wounds close or scab over until they're clean. I'll make a poultice for that hind leg and help you put it on. Now that she'll let us get close to her, we can help her a lot."

"The thing to do is see that she eats," said Rob. "Keep up her strength."

But he himself would not go near her. "She won't pull out of it," he said. "I don't want to see her or think about her."

Kennie and his mother nursed the filly. The big poultice was bandaged on the hind leg. It drew out much poisoned matter, and Flicka felt better and was able to stand again.

She watched for Kennie now and followed him like a dog, hopping on three legs, holding up the right hind leg with its huge knob of bandage in a comical fashion.

"Dad, Flicka's my friend now; she likes me," said Ken.

His father looked at him. "I'm glad of that, son. It's a fine thing to have a horse for a friend."

Kennie found a nicer place for her. In the lower pasture the brook ran over cool stones. There was a grassy bank, the size of a corral, almost on a level with the water. Here she could lie softly, eat grass, drink fresh running water. From the grass, a twenty-foot hill sloped up, crested with over-hanging trees. She was enclosed, as it were, in a green, open-air nursery.

Kennie carried her oats morning and evening. She would watch for him to come, eyes and ears pointed to the hill. And one evening Ken, still some distance off, came to a stop and a wide grin spread over his face. He had heard her nicker. She had caught sight of him coming and was calling to him!

He placed the box of oats under her nose, and she ate while

he stood beside her, his hand smoothing the satin-soft skin under her mane. It had a nap as deep as plush. He played with her long, cream-colored tresses, arranged her forelock neatly between her eyes. She was a bit dish-faced, like an Arab, with eyes set far apart. He lightly groomed and brushed her while she stood turning her head to him whichever way he went.

He spoiled her. Soon she would not step to the stream to drink but he must hold a bucket for her. And she would drink, then lift her dripping muzzle, rest it on the shoulder of his blue chambray shirt, her golden eyes dreaming off into the distance, then daintily dip her mouth and drink again.

When she turned her head to the south and pricked her ears and stood tense and listening, Ken knew she heard the other colts galloping on the upland.

"You'll go back there someday, Flicka," he whispered. "You'll be three, and I'll be eleven. You'll be so strong you won't know I'm on your back, and we'll fly like the wind. We'll stand on the very top where we can look over the whole world and smell the snow from Neversummer Range. Maybe we'll see antelope. . . ."

This was the happiest month of Kennie's life.

With the morning Flicka always had new strength and would hop three-legged up the hill to stand broadside to the early sun, as horses love to do.

The moment Ken woke he'd go to the window and see her there, and when he was dressed and at his table studying, he sat so that he could raise his head and see Flicka.

After breakfast she would be waiting at the gate for him and the box of oats, and for Nell McLaughlin with fresh bandages and buckets of disinfectant. All three would go together to the brook, Flicka hopping along ahead of them as if she were leading the way.

But Rob McLaughlin would not look at her.

One day all the wounds were swollen again. Presently they

opened, one by one, and Kennie and his mother made more poultices.

Still the little filly climbed the hill in the early morning and ran about on three legs. Then she began to go down in flesh and almost overnight wasted away to nothing. Every rib showed; the glossy hide was dull and brittle and was pulled over the skeleton as if she were a dead horse.

Gus said, "It's de fever. It burns up her flesh. If you could stop de fever she might get vell."

McLaughlin was standing in his window one morning and saw the little skeleton hopping about three-legged in the sunshine, and he said, "That's the end. I won't have a thing like that on my place."

Kennie had to understand that Flicka had not been getting well all this time; she had been slowly dying.

"She still eats her oats," he said mechanically.

They were all sorry for Ken. Nell McLaughlin stopped disinfecting and dressing the wounds. "It's no use, Ken," she said gently, "you know Flicka's going to die, don't you?"

"Yes, Mother."

Ken stopped eating. Howard said, "Ken doesn't eat anything anymore. Don't he have to eat his dinner, Mother?"

But Nell answered, "Leave him alone."

Because the shooting of wounded animals is all in the day's work on the western plains, and sickening to everyone, Rob's voice, when he gave the order to have Flicka shot, was as flat as if he had been telling Gus to kill a chicken for dinner.

"Here's the Marlin, Gus. Pick out a time when Ken's not around and put the filly out of her misery."

Gus took the rifle. *"Ja,* boss . . ."

Ever since Ken had known that Flicka was to be shot he had kept his eye on the rack which held the firearms. His father allowed no firearms in the bunkhouse. The gun rack was in the dining room of the ranch house, and going through it to the kitchen three times a day for meals, Ken's eye scanned the weapons to make sure that they were all there.

That night they were not all there. The Marlin rifle was missing.

When Kennie saw that he stopped walking. He felt dizzy. He kept staring at the gun rack, telling himself that it surely was there—he counted again and again—he couldn't see clearly . . .

Then he felt an arm across his shoulders and heard his father's voice.

"I know, son. Some things are awful hard to take. We just have to take 'em. I have to, too."

Kennie got hold of his father's hand and held on. It helped steady him.

Finally he looked up. Rob looked down and smiled at him and gave him a little shake and squeeze. Ken managed a smile too.

"All right now?"

"All right, Dad."

They walked in to supper together.

Ken even ate a little. But Nell looked thoughtfully at the ashen color of his face and at the little pulse that was beating in the side of his neck.

After supper he carried Flicka her oats, but he had to coax her and she would only eat a little. She stood with her head hanging, but when he stroked it and talked to her she pressed her face into his chest and was content. He could feel the burning heat of her body. It didn't seem possible that anything so thin could be alive.

Presently Kennie saw Gus come into the pasture carrying the Marlin. When he saw Ken he changed his direction and sauntered along as if he was out to shoot some cottontails.

Ken ran to him. "When are you going to do it, Gus?"

"Ay was goin' down soon now, before it got dark . . ."

"Gus, don't do it tonight. Wait till morning. Just one more night, Gus."

"Vell, in de morning den, but it got to be done, Ken. Yer fader gives de order."

"I know. I won't say anything more."

An hour after the family had gone to bed Ken got up and put on his clothes. It was a warm moonlit night. He ran down to the brook, calling softly, "Flicka! Flicka!"

But Flicka did not answer with a little nicker; and she was not in the nursery nor hopping about the pasture. Ken hunted for an hour.

At last he found her down the creek, lying in the water. Her head had been on the bank, but as she lay there the current of the stream had sucked and pulled at her, and she had had no strength to resist; and little by little her head had slipped down until when Ken got there only the muzzle was resting on the bank, and the body and legs were swinging in the stream.

Kennie slid into the water, sitting on the bank, and he hauled at her head. But she was heavy, and the current dragged like a weight; and he began to sob because he had no strength to draw her out.

Then he found a leverage for his heels against some rocks in the bed of the stream and he braced himself against these and pulled with all his might; and her head came up onto his knees, and he held it cradled in his arms.

He was glad that she had died of her own accord, in the cool water, under the moon, instead of being shot by Gus. Then, putting his face close to hers, and looking searchingly into her eyes, he saw that she was alive and looking back at him.

And then he burst out crying and hugged her and said, "Oh, my little Flicka, my little Flicka."

The long night passed.

The moon slid slowly across the heavens.

The water rippled over Kennie's legs and over Flicka's body. And gradually the heat and fever went out of her. And the cool running water washed and washed her wounds.

When Gus went down in the morning with the rifle they hadn't moved. There they were, Kennie sitting in water over his thighs and hips, with Flicka's head in his arms.

Gus seized Flicka by the head and hauled her out on the grassy bank and then, seeing that Kennie couldn't move, cold and stiff and half-paralyzed as he was, lifted him in his arms and carried him to the house.

"Gus," said Ken through chattering teeth, "don't shoot her, Gus."

"It ain't fur me to say, Ken. You know dat."

"But the fever's left her, Gus."

"Ay wait a little, Ken . . ."

Rob McLaughlin drove to Laramie to get the doctor, for Ken was in violent chills that would not stop. His mother had him in bed wrapped in hot blankets when they got back.

He looked at his father imploringly as the doctor shook down the thermometer.

"She might get well now, Dad. The fever's left her. It went out of her when the moon went down."

"All right, son. Don't worry. Gus'll feed her, morning and night, as long as she's—"

"As long as I can't do it," finished Ken happily.

The doctor put the thermometer in his mouth and told him to keep it shut.

All day Gus went about his work, thinking of Flicka. He had not been back to look at her. He had been given no more orders. If she was alive the order to shoot her was still in effect. But Kennie was ill, McLaughlin making his second trip to town taking the doctor home, and would not be back till long after dark.

After their supper in the bunkhouse Gus and Tim walked down to the brook. They did not speak as they approached the filly, lying stretched out flat on the grassy bank, but their eyes were straining at her to see if she was dead or alive.

She raised her head as they reached her.

"By the powers!" exclaimed Tim. "There she is!"

She dropped her head, raised it again, and moved her legs and became tense as if struggling to rise. But to do so she must use her right hind leg to brace herself against the earth. That was the damaged leg, and at the first bit of pressure with it she gave up and fell back.

"We'll swing her onto the other side," said Tim. "Then she can help herself."

"*Ja . . .*"

Standing behind her, they leaned over, grabbed hold of her left legs, front and back, and gently hauled her over. Flicka was as lax and willing as a puppy, but the moment she found herself lying on her right side, she began to scramble, braced herself with her good left leg, and tried to rise.

"Yee whiz!" said Gus. "She got plenty strength yet."

"Hi!" cheered Tim. "She's up!"

But Flicka wavered, slid down again, and lay flat. This time she gave notice that she would not try again by heaving a deep sigh and closing her eyes.

Gus took his pipe out of his mouth and thought it over. Orders or no orders, he would try to save the filly. Ken had gone too far to be let down.

"Ay'm goin' to rig a blanket sling fur her, Tim, and get her on her feet, and keep her up."

There was bright moonlight to work by. They brought down the posthole digger and set two aspen poles deep into the ground either side of the filly, then, with ropes attached to the blanket, hoisted her by a pulley.

Not at all disconcerted, she rested comfortably in the blanket under her belly, touched her feet on the ground, and reached for the bucket of water Gus held for her.

Kennie was sick a long time. He nearly died. But Flicka picked up. Every day Gus passed the word to Nell, who carried it to Ken. "She's cleaning up her oats." "She's out of the sling." "She bears a little weight on the bad leg."

Tim declared it was a real miracle. They argued about it, eating their supper.

"Na," said Gus. "It was de cold water, washin' de fever outa her. And more dan dat—it was Ken—you tink it don't count? All night dot boy sits dere and says, 'Hold on, Flicka, Ay'm here wid you. Ay'm standin' by, two of us togedder' . . ."

Tim stared at Gus without answering, while he thought it over. In the silence a coyote yapped far off on the plains, and the wind made a rushing sound high up in the jack pines on the hill.

Gus filled his pipe.

"Sure," said Tim finally. "Sure. That's it."

Then came the day when Rob McLaughlin stood smiling at the foot of Kennie's bed and said, "Listen! Hear your friend?"

Ken listened and heard Flicka's high, eager whinny.

"She don't spend much time by the brook anymore. She's up at the gate of the corral half the time, nickering for you."

"For me!"

Rob wrapped a blanket around the boy and carried him out to the corral gate.

Kennie gazed at Flicka. There was a look of marveling in his eyes. He felt as if he had been living in a world where everything was dreadful and hurting but awfully real; and

134

this couldn't be real; this was all soft and happy, nothing to struggle over or worry about or fight for anymore. Even his father was proud of him! He could feel it in the way Rob's big arms held him. It was all like a dream and far away. He couldn't, yet, get close to anything.

But Flicka—Flicka—alive, well, pressing up to him, recognizing him, nickering . . .

Kennie put out a hand—weak and white—and laid it on her face. His thin little fingers straightened her forelock the way he used to do, while Rob looked at the two with a strange expression about his mouth and a glow in his eyes that was not often there.

"She's still poor, Dad, but she's on four legs now."

"She's picking up."

Ken turned his face up, suddenly remembering. "Dad! She did get gentled, didn't she?"

"Gentle—as a kitten . . ."

They put a cot down by the brook for Ken, and boy and filly got well together.

*Acclaimed fantasy writer Shirley Rousseau Murphy
has also written a number of realistic books about horses—
not surprising as her father was a professional horseman
who worked with hunters and jumpers, and who even
trained horses for work in Hollywood movies.*

DEAR PONY

This right, bright pony
Eyes wild, coat tawny
Outwitting people is his game
Disaster is his proper name

Kicks the groom who brings him hay
Breaks his rope and wheels away
Jumps the fence, won't come to me
Avoids all capture skillfully

Ears back, expression mean
Stubbornest I've ever seen
And if he's caught he's not contrite
Turn your back and he will bite

When I saddle him, why then
Kicks my stirrup, bites again
And always bucks on mornings cool
Dumps me so I look a fool

But he, upon the roughest trail
Is skilled where other horses fail

Over fences, leaping logs
Past the meanest barking dogs

Through the thick and tangled wood
Crossing rivers' widest ford
Along thin ridges skillfully
Dodging chuckholes carefully

Then he's safe and sure and right
Every challenge, his delight
I want no other, meeker made
Not for any price would trade

Crazy mane and swinging rear
Sassy, spoiled and very dear
Eyes sharp, coat tawny
He's my right, bright pony.

—Shirley Rousseau Murphy

ary Stanton grew up in Hawaii, went to college in Minnesota, and now makes her home in upstate New York, where she runs a business communications firm, raises horses, and writes novels like The Heavenly Horse from the Outermost West *and* Piper at the Gate. *As this sensitive short story shows, she understands not only horses, but the people who love them.*

$\mathcal{S}$ UNRISE

Mary Stanton

"**I'll bet that's** for me, and I'll bet it's one of my sisters," my stepmother said when the phone rang. She does that all the time, trying to make me think she knows who's calling even before she picks up the phone. She says it's love that lets her know, and my dad laughs like a fool with a dopey smile on his face and calls it ESP. I call it just plain guessing. Except that she guessed right for once. It was Alicia, her youngest sister, who my stepmother always tries to make me call Aunt even though she isn't.

"Well," said my stepmother, coming back into the living room after she'd hung up the phone. "In a way that was for Jeri."

My dad made a "that's nice" kind of noise and continued with his reading. My stepmother came and sat on the couch where I was watching TV.

She put her hand on my shoulder and I politely moved it out of the way. She doesn't even look like my mother, for one thing. She's too young. And she makes me mad. For instance, she makes these cookies and says they're just for me in a drippy voice that makes me sick. Did I ask for those cookies? No, I did not. Did I ask her to come and live here with us after Mom left? I did not.

"That was Aunt Alicia," she said, as though I didn't know that she'd guessed it. Before the phone even *rang* probably.

"So?" I said, bored.

"She's going off to college in a month."

"Yeah." Alicia is ten years younger than my stepmother and only six years older than me, so it would feel weird to call her my aunt even if I wanted to.

"You remember Sunrise, don't you?"

Sunrise is this horse Alicia owns, which is the only cool thing about my stepmother, that she has a younger sister with a horse.

"She can't keep Sunrise at college, of course. And she's getting too busy with other things to be able to spend time with Sunrise; horses take a lot of work. She wants you to have her."

They were showing that commercial on TV, the one where the black lady cries when her son calls from college just to say, "I love you, Mom." It's a stupid commercial, but I like it anyway.

"We could make a stall out of the garden shed," said my stepmother. "We could fence in the backyard."

My father dropped his book. "A horse in the backyard?"

"We have three acres here, Willy. There's enough room." She put her hand on my shoulder again. "Would you like that, Jeri? A horse of your own?"

The commercial had changed to the one where the little kid is rolling on the grass with these puppies crawling all over him. The kid laughs and laughs in the commercial.

"I guess," I said.

My mom, who lives in New Jersey with this guy who works for IBM, would have just died to see what my dad did with the back lawn. First he ripped out all the rose bushes and planted them in the front yard, where they looked weird. Then he put up a wooden fence. He made me help him clean out the garden shed. I twisted my ankle when we were carrying out the picnic table he'd made before the divorce, so I couldn't help him finish. My stepmother did, though. She probably wanted to see all that stuff thrown out. It was from when Mom and Dad were together, and I don't think she wanted the reminders around anymore. We rented this huge automatic hammer and broke up the concrete floor and made it all dirt. Dad said that horses need soft ground to stand on and that their bones get stiff if they sleep or stand on concrete.

The shed looked pretty cool when he finished. We had a front gate and a back door. When the back door was open, Sunrise could go in and out whenever she wanted to. We put in a feed box with a lock on it for the oats and shelves for all the stuff this horse would need. My stepmother and I went to a tack shop and got a hoof pick and plastic buckets for water and oats, and some boots for me to wear when I rode Sunrise in the backyard.

Alicia visited the day when the hay and straw were delivered. I couldn't tell the difference between the bales; it all looked like weeds to me.

"The straw is made from the stems of oats," Alicia said. "It's thick and yellow-colored. The hay is made from dried grass and it's thin and greenish brown. You use the straw for bedding and the hay for feed." She smiled and looked around the garden shed. "I think this looks great, don't you? Sunrise will love it here."

"I guess so."

Alicia isn't too bad, even if she is six years older than I am.

She's not very tall, and she's skinny with long blond hair. We looked around the shed together. The hay was stacked in one corner all the way to the ceiling. It smelled good, as if the sun had dried in it.

"You'll have to feed her twice a day," said Alicia. "And be sure to brush out her coat every day, and change her water so that it's fresh and sweet." She came close and looked at me with her greeny eyes. "Sunrise is very special, you know. If you give her good care, you'll find out just how special she is. But you'll have to learn a lot about keeping her stall clean and taking care of her if she gets sick, and feeding and watering her every day. Nina (that's my stepmother) knows a lot about horses. She can help you take care of Sunrise."

"I got a book from the library," I said.

"About horses? That's terrific. But there's a lot about horses that you learn from just being around them. Each horse is different. And you'll have to discover just how different Sunrise is on your own."

Sunrise came that Saturday in a long trailer. Alicia backed her out of the trailer and down a ramp and she stood in the sunshine. She looked like a sunrise, all glowy gold, with a dark mane and tail. She had beautiful eyes, the color of chocolate. But she was big, bigger than I thought she'd be. She clopped down the driveway to the garden shed with Alicia leading her on a rope. She even sounded big.

I hung on the bars outside her stall and looked at her for a while. She dipped her nose into the water bucket and shook her head so that the water flew around her face. She ate a few bites of the hay I'd put there.

Then my stepmother walked into the shed. Sunrise raised her head and whickered.

"She's so beautiful," my stepmother said. She looked at me as though she was expecting me to gush on about the horse too. But I just nodded.

"Alicia's saddle might be a little large for you," she said

after a while. "So you might want to try riding her bareback for the first couple of months. I can teach you, if you like."

Bareback? On that huge thing? She had to be kidding.

After a while she said, "Do you want to know anything else about picking out her feet or brushing her down?"

"I got a book from the library."

"So you did. Did Alicia tell you that there are things to learn about horses that never get written down? That each horse is special in its own way?"

"I guess."

"One of the things I know about Sunrise is that she will obey you even if you are a little nervous about being around her. She's very calm."

"I am *not* nervous," I said, getting mad.

"Well, anyone would be," said my stepmother. "She *is* big and she *is* a horse in what used to be a perfectly good garden shed. It must seem strange to see her here."

And then my stepmother, who's never had any guts at all before as far as I could tell, unlatched the stall door and walked right in front of that horse.

Sunrise snorted and stuck her nose into my stepmother's hand. "Shh-shh," my stepmother said, just as she did when I'd had the flu at the start of school last year. "Jeri, come and see how soft her coat is."

"I can see from here," I said. To tell you the truth, I wasn't just nervous about this horse, I was dead scared. But I would rather have had three teeth drilled for cavities than let my stepmother know that.

"You can't *feel* from there." She put one hand under Sunrise's nose, and the other on her cheek and the horse moved with her and they walked right over to where I was clinging to the stall wall, with my hands and feet sticking through the spaces between the boards.

"Put your hand here, on her neck."

I did. It was weird. I could feel the gold hair. It felt like the silky blouses my mother liked to wear.

"Put your hand here, over her heart."

I had to reach over to do this, so I slipped off the boards and into the stall next to this horse.

"If you put your ear to her side, you'll hear her heart beating."

And there it was, the warm sound of this horse living beneath my ear. I felt a touch on my hair, like a kiss.

She looked at me, with her chocolate-colored eyes and she *saw* me. I knew she did. She knew who I was.

"You can tell this horse things you'd never want to tell anyone else," said my stepmother. "She'll keep your secrets and maybe tell you some of her own."

Here I was beginning to think my stepmother had some sense and she goes and says something dumb like that. She finally left Sunrise and me alone. I brushed my horse with a soft brush. She seemed to like it.

I opened the back door to the stall the next morning and Sunrise ran out into the pasture we'd made for her. She rolled in the grass, her legs waving in the air, and then she ran around and around the fence, kicking up her heels and squealing. The book I'd gotten from the library had a chart called "Barn Routine," and I'd copied it out onto notebook paper. The first thing you do in a "Barn Routine" is turn the horse out and muck out. "Mucking out" means picking up the totally gross piles of manure and neatly disposing of them. I put them into a blue plastic manure bucket. You are then supposed to turn over the straw with the pitchfork, looking for places where the horse has peed. So I did that. Then you are supposed to give them water, hay, and oats, in that order. Otherwise, it gives them the colic.

I filled the water bucket after scrubbing out the green goo

in the bucket from where Sunrise had dunked her hay. Then I piled two leaves of hay in the manger. A leaf of hay is not what you think; it's the parts of a bale that stay together when you snip the baling twine. I wasn't too sure about the oats. You feed oats in different amounts for when a horse is under light, medium, or heavy work. I figured that Sunrise was under light work, since she wasn't on a racetrack or anything, so I gave her one scoop of oats in the feed bucket. When she heard the oats rattle into the feed bucket, she ran right into the stall and I got out of the way. She ate the oats in a nice way, taking a few bites and chewing. Then she licked the bucket like a little kid. It was pretty hilarious. She looked at me when she'd licked the bucket clean, and I said, "More oats, girl?" figuring maybe I guessed wrong and she was under medium work. So I gave her another scoop. She ate those in a nice way, too, but nowhere near as fast, so I figured that she maybe was under light work after all.

She ate her hay, chewing away with a very nice sound, almost like rocking in a chair, rock-rock, chew-chew. It was great.

"I do have a secret," I said. Sunrise flicked one ear back and swung her head to look at me.

"My stepmother hates me." I said this in a very calm way, but in a whisper, since it was a secret.

"And I hate my stepmother. Nothing's been right since she came."

Sunrise walked through the straw to where I was standing and nudged me in the chest. If she hadn't done that, I wouldn't have cried—at least, not so hard. But I did. I cried and Sunrise nibbled at my hair, and when I put my arms around her neck, I cried harder.

Crying is a weird thing, like getting the knots out of your hair after you've stuck your head out of the window of the car when your Dad's driving fast. It hurts to get the comb through at first, but then things feel smooth. I felt as if I'd combed out some king-size knots when I finished crying. I sniffed back, which I'm not supposed to do since it rots your stomach or something, and decided that I'd told Sunrise the biggest secret I had, and that was enough for the morning.

I opened the stall door to the shed and pulled out the plastic manure bucket. Dad had said that the best way to dispose of the manure neatly was to make a pile near the compost in the garden. So I tugged at the bucket, and it slid across the dirt floor and into the yard. I carried the bucket to the compost and set it down with a thump. Then I felt a nudge in my back. I turned around. Sunrise had followed me right out the open stall door.

"Go back to your stall, girl."

She started grabbing at the green grass, as though there weren't enough of the stuff in her own pasture. I looked around, my heart thumping. There was no fence here to keep Sunrise in, and she could walk right out of the yard and into the road. There was a lot of traffic there. She could get killed.

"Easy, girl." I grabbed at her halter, and she swung her head and backed away. She looked around and I could almost see her realize she was free, that she could run over the grass, and I'd never see her again. I grabbed at her halter again, and she backed up and trotted way to the edge of the road, ears pricked up, listening.

"Here, Sunrise. Here, girl." I ran behind her, but each time I got anywhere near close enough to catch her, she moved away.

My insides were churning. I was terrified. What if something happened to her?

"Jeri," my dad called from the back porch. "Jeri, your horse is out."

This was probably the dumbest thing anyone has ever said to me.

"Will, you go around to the mare's left side." My step-

145

mother came down the porch with an apple in her hand. "Jeri, you go around to the right. I'll go out in the road. Don't come up behind her, or she'll just move away from you."

It worked, although by now I was crying again and I was such a revolting mess that I was surprised that dumb horse didn't take off down the road like a train. But we caught her and Sunrise ate the apple my stepmother gave me and then shoved her nose in my hand for more.

"She's new here, you know," said my stepmother. "She just doesn't know where to go or what to do."

"That's not it and you know it," I said, sniffing back again. But I didn't say the rest of what I was feeling—that when I had told Sunrise my secret, it made her so disgusted she wanted to get away from me.

"Jeri, the horse is all right," said my father sharply. "Take her back to her stall and stop crying. You're all right, and nobody's hurt. Just don't leave the front stall door open so she can get out. Horses don't know anything about roads and traffic."

I put Sunrise back in her stall. I needed to be alone for a little while. But my stepmother followed me into the shed. I got mad. Why couldn't she just leave me alone? "Go away!" I screamed. "I hate you! And you hate me! And you made my horse hate me!" It was all her fault, because she was the one who brought this horse here in the first place and who told me I could tell this horse anything and the horse wouldn't care.

"She ran away from me because she thinks I'm a jerk!" I said.

"No, Jeri, you're wrong," my stepmother said. "Do you want to know what Sunrise is thinking?"

I looked up.

"She thinks of grass like velvet under a summer sun. Of clear water and a breeze to lift her mane from her neck. Of a ride up a flowery hill with you on her back, into a daisy-filled

meadow. This is what Sunrise is thinking. Put your ear against her heart and your chest against her side, and she'll tell you."

I put my cheek against the mare's side because I was tired and not because my stepmother told me to.

And something happened. I stretched my arms around her golden hide and saw what Sunrise saw, and felt what she felt. The sweet-tasting grass tickled my nose. The hot sun was shining on my back. The cool breeze stirred my mane.

There was more than that. There was a feeling in the back of my neck, around my ribs and chest like a great warm blanket. Sunrise and I were wrapped in this blanket together.

I found out something, too. I looked at my stepmother and she smiled at me.

"*You* used to own Sunrise," I said.

"I hope you don't mind. She didn't belong to me, you know. I belonged to her. There's a difference. Sunrise is the sort of horse you belong to for a while, until you're older, like Alicia or me, and then she moves on. That's why you can tell her anything you want to. A horse like Sunrise is more than just a horse—she's special—and she'll care for you. You belong to her and you will until you're ready to leave her."

I wound my hands in Sunrise's mane. "That'll be the day," I said.

I didn't look at my stepmother. "The secret I told her wasn't a true one, anyway. I expect she knew that."

My stepmother had her I-hope-I-know-who's-on-the-phone look, and I didn't mind at all, this time.

"I love you too, Jeri," she said.

And Sunrise nuzzled my ear.

T he myths and legends of northern Europe are filled with such mighty steeds as Odin's great eight-legged Sleipnir and the war horses of the Valkyries. From Norway comes this tale about a giant horse named Dapplegrim. The tale was first translated from Norwegian into English by George W. Dasent; I have retold the first part of it for this volume.

DAPPLEGRIM

Retold by Bruce Coville

Dapplegrim was a horse, and the greatest horse there ever was, if you take greatness to mean size, though he was wonderful in other ways as well. He lived once on a time and long ago, and this is the story of how he came to grow, and the amazing things he did thereafter.

The story begins with a handsome lad who had eleven brothers. His parents were wealthy and had many servants, so there was little enough for the boy to do at home. This made him restless, and despite his parents' objections, he wandered off to see the world.

Eventually he came to a city, where there was much weeping and wailing. The old women were beating their breasts, and the young men tearing their hair. When the lad asked what was the matter a woman explained that only yesterday a horrible troll had stolen the King's daughter, who was more beautiful than sunrise over a lake. He had carried her off to his cave, which was in a sheer cliff as straight as a stare and

149

smooth as a sheet of glass. As might be expected, the King was wild with grief, and had offered half the kingdom to whomever might bring back his daughter. But our lad was a gentle soul, and this did not seem like a thing that he could do. So he wandered on, and eventually wandered right back to his home. But in all that wandering time he never forgot the story of the King's daughter.

Now when our lad arrived home, he found that his parents had died. His brothers had already shared out all that the old folks owned, and so there was nothing left for the lad.

"Shan't I have anything at all then, out of our parents' wealth?" he cried.

His brothers grumbled that with all his wandering, for all they knew he had been dead as well. But the oldest brother, who was not a bad sort, mentioned that there were twelve mares up on the hill that they had not yet shared out. "You may have those if you wish," he said. And the lad, who loved horses, was well pleased.

When he climbed to the top of the hill, he found that each of the mares had a foal at her side, and one mare had a large dapple gray colt as well, with a coat so sleek that it seemed to catch the very rays of the sun.

"Well, aren't you a one," said the lad, admiring the colt.

"Yes, but I'll be one better if you will only take away all the others so that I may have the milk from all the mares for another year. For no way else can I be what I should be."

The lad was so astonished by this remarkable colt that he did what it asked. When he came back a year later he found that once more each of the mares had a tiny new foal at her side. But the dappled foal had grown until it was so large he could barely mount it.

"Well, you were true to your word," said the lad. "And now you shall come with me."

"Ah no," said the colt. "Only let me run and nurse from all

the other mares for another year, and you'll see what I may become."

And as the first year had been so successful, once again the lad took away the other foals, and left Dapple to nurse on all the mares. And when he returned the following summer each mare had her foal, but the dappled colt was so huge that the lad could stand under its head and not reach its chin even if he jumped.

"Well, you were true to your word," said the lad. "And now you shall come with me."

"Ah no," said Dapple. "By what I am, you can see what I may become, just as I promised. But let me stay another year, and I will become all that I can."

Well, this rather confused the lad, but he agreed to let Dapple stay, and rounding up the new foals, he left his remarkable horse on the hill to nurse from the twelve mares. And when he returned a year later, astonished he was indeed, for so tall and sleek and sturdy had Dapple become that the horse had to lie down in the grass before the lad could mount him. And when Dapple stood up again, the young man felt as if he were looking down from such a great height that he might almost have been flying.

"And now, at last, I am ready to leave the hill," said Dapplegrim.

"That is just as well," said the lad, "for if you were to grow another time I don't know what I should do with you!"

They went riding down the hill, where the brothers came out of the house and laughed and clapped to see the enormous horse. And then the lad said that if they would provide shoes and saddle and bridle for the beast, they could have the twelve mares on the hill, and the twelve foals they had with them—but only if the bridle and saddle were the grandest ever seen.

The brothers thought this a fair trade, and soon enough the lad was off and away on his great horse. The golden saddle and the golden bridle shone like fire in the sun, and as they galloped off the earth shook beneath them, and the stones that flew up from Dapple's hooves shot so high they pierced the clouds and made them rain.

"Now," said the horse, when they had gone a way and decided to walk for a bit, "it is time we decided what to do for you, and my suggestion is that we head for the King's palace, and see what we can see."

This was fine with the lad, and so off they went.

Well, the King happened to be standing at a window, gazing toward Troll Mountain, when our lad and Dapplegrim came riding into sight.

"Such a horse I have never seen!" cried the King in astonishment, and with his men trailing behind him, he went out to meet the lad.

Dapplegrim said nothing, for he would speak only to the lad. But the boy said, as Dapplegrim had instructed him, that if the King wished him to stay he must have a good stable and good fodder for his horse. Well, that was no problem as far as the King was concerned, for he was eager to have this great horse in the stable. But it was a problem with the other knights, for their horses were put out to make room for Dapplegrim. This made the knights angry, and by way of revenge they went to the King and said that they had heard the lad boasting that he could rescue the Princess, if only he had a mind to do so.

This made the King angry, for he felt that the lad was holding out on him. So he called him to the throne room and said that if he could rescue the Princess then he had best do so right quickly, and play no games about it. And if he did, then he should marry her and have half the kingdom, as the King had promised. But if he refused, then he would be killed, and that would be the end of it.

The lad protested over and over that he had never said any such thing, but the King refused to hear him, so set was his mind on getting back his daughter, whom he loved more dearly than anything.

So there was no choice but that the lad must go face the troll, and mighty unhappy about it he was, too.

When the lad went to the stable to talk to Dapplegrim that night his face was so mournful that the horse asked him what was wrong. But when he told all that had happened, Dapplegrim only laughed, and said that together they would save the Princess. "But first you must have me well shod," said the horse. "Ask for twelve pounds of iron, and twelve of steel, and one smith to hammer and one to hold."

When all was done as had been asked, the lad and the horse set off to save the Princess.

Long they traveled, and longer still, till they came to Troll Mountain, where the Princess was kept prisoner. When he saw the mountainside, our lad's heart sank to his toes, for there seemed no way to climb it. But Dapplegrim was cheerful, and said, "Only hold on, for I have not been shod so well for nothing."

Then backing up, the enormous horse galloped toward the cliff, and just when the lad thought they should dash their brains out against the rock, Dapplegrim went clambering up that sheer wall. But they had only got up a bit when his forelegs slipped and down they came with a crash that shook the mountain.

Not a bit discouraged, Dapplegrim backed up and tried again. His hooves pounded against the earth like falling comets. The stones shot out behind him like rockets. And just when the lad thought they should dash their brains out against the cliff up they went and higher still, till they were almost at the cave. But then one foreleg slipped, and down they fell with a crash that shook the sky above.

"Third time the charm," said Dapplegrim, and backing up even farther, he went pounding toward the mountain like an

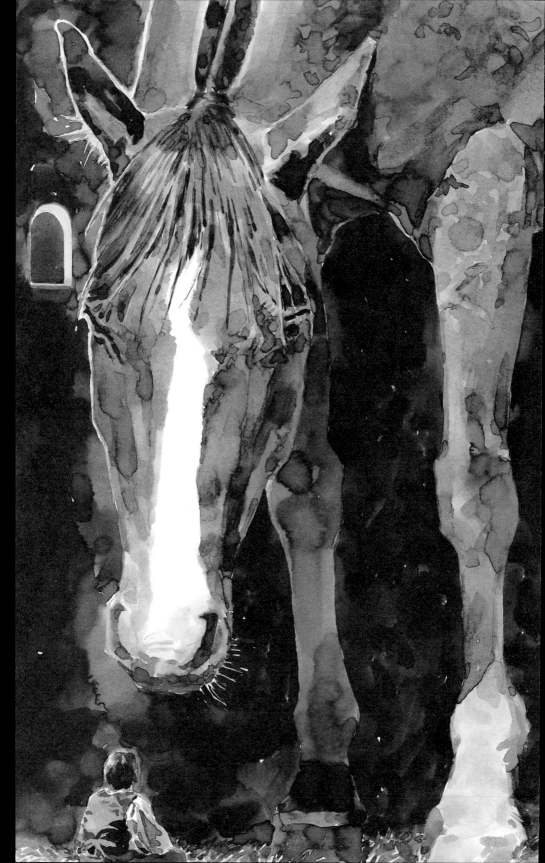

arrow from a bow. The earth shook beneath them and the stones from his hooves flew over the clouds. And just when the lad thought that this time they must die against the cliff, up they went and higher than ever, straight up that glass smooth wall until they were over the edge and into the cave of the troll, which was bigger inside than it was out, with a ceiling as high as a cathedral, and walls as wide as a lake.

But then what a fright they had, for the troll himself was as tall as a tree and as ugly as a lie and meaner than a winter storm. His eyes were like pits of fire and his moss-green hair hung in tangles around his knees. Roaring with anger, the troll stood up and lifted his club, which was made from a great oak.

"Now hold on!" said Dapplegrim. For on the far side of the troll they could see the Princess, looking more beautiful than a sunrise over a lake. Then Dapplegrim circled wide, and his pounding hooves shook stones from the ceiling. But he moved so fast that the lad was able to snatch the Princess into the saddle before the troll had raised his club as far as his shoulders.

"Now faster still!" called the lad, holding the Princess to him. Then out they shot, and down they slid, and so rapidly did they move that it wasn't until they reached the base of the mountain that they heard the troll's club strike the floor.

The Princess was so glad to be rescued, and the lad was so handsome and gentle, that she fell in love with him quite on the spot.

"And isn't that the way of it," said Dapplegrim, "even though I did all the work." But he was not displeased, for he was fond of the lad, and wanted only his happiness.

And so they rode toward home. But that was not the end of their adventures, not by half, for though the best ending to a story is "they lived happily ever after," few there are who are happy without something going on. Surely the lad and his lady were such, and the wonders and troubles they found when they returned home would make another tale. But see, my thread has run out, so I can say no more.

Jennifer Roberson has lived with and around horses for much of her life. In fact, she was once Miss Rodeo Arizona. She still lives in Arizona with her husband Mark O'Green (who designs computer games) and several pets.

Though she usually writes fantasy novels, Jennifer is fascinated by the real history of the Scythians—an ancient people who lived northeast of the Black Sea and are said to have been the world's first horsemen. While reading about these people, Jennifer came across the true incident—the startling of a hare—that forms the turning point of this thrilling adventure story.

T O

$\mathcal{R}$IDE

T H E

$\mathcal{S}$EA OF $\mathcal{G}$RASS

Jennifer Roberson

It was thunder without the storm. No rain, no wind, no clouds. Just a thunder that filled the skies, spilling over the rim of the world.

Transfixed by the sound, Sashi caught her breath. The noise filled her with longing and a wild exhilaration. "They're coming," she whispered intently, then laughed aloud for joy.

Thunder swallowed her world, filling eyes and ears with horses; tens and twenties of horses, breasting through the hip-high grass as they poured out of the setting sun. Duns and bays and browns, like a river of living earth.

"They're coming," she said again, and the river rushed, sweeping by her.

Grass lay down before the horses, crushed under unshod hooves. Dust rose to ride the air, much as men rode the horses. The Greeks called them *centaurs,* creatures both horse and man, but Sashi knew better than Greeks. She *should;* she was Scythian. Horses were in her blood, but not a part of her body.

She heard shouts and laughter and swearing; the rattle of gold-plated gear; the snorts and squeals of horses, warning others from drawing too near.

Sashi gloried in the dust, in the noise, in the smells of hoof-churned earth and grass. But mostly what she loved was the scent of steppes-born horses.

Tears sprang to her eyes. "If only *I* could have one. One all my *own.*"

But even as she said it, Sashi knew better. Scythian girls and women rode, but in wagons, not on horses. Horses were left to the men, and the boys who would take their places.

"Sashi! *Sashi*—come back to the tent. The Sarmatians will run over you."

The call came from Uta, her mother—who didn't, Sashi felt, understand at all.

Sarmatians, not Scythians. Another tribe had come, answering the invitation of her people to join in defense of the steppes, now invaded by the Persian army led by King Darius himself.

"Sarmatians," she said aloud, staring out at the river of horses.

"Sashi! Will you *please* get out of the way?"

Sluggishly, she moved. She knew her mother was right.

Horses set to running caught fire from their riders, and although none would run down a person on purpose, sometimes they had no choice. Better to give them room now and go out to see them later.

Sashi turned and saw her mother waiting impatiently. Uta had put on festive clothing to celebrate the joining of the tribes against the Persian invaders. She wore a soft leather caftan patterned with bright blue thread, and high beaded boots. Gold shone in her ears; she had put on her favorite earrings in honor of the feast. Beyond Uta were tents, tens and twenties of them made of brightly dyed felt, adorned with numerous patterns of real and imagined animals. Sashi's favorite was the blue gryphon with widespread wings.

"Come." Now Uta spoke more kindly; perhaps she *did* understand. "It's time for you to put on your best caftan, and the colored glass beads your father got from the Greeks last year."

Sashi nodded, glanced back at the Sarmatians for one last look, and stopped dead in her tracks. "Women," she said in shock. "Girls and women—*riding!*"

"Sarmatians," her mother said, as if it explained everything.

To Sashi it explained nothing, except that Sarmatian girls could ride horses instead of wagons. "They're riding with the *men!*"

"They're different from us," Uta said. "Now, will you come along? We're feasting them tonight . . . you can stare at them later."

Sashi did as asked, but amazement accompanied her.

The feast was the best Sashi could remember, and certainly the noisiest. There was meat in abundance—mutton, beef, boar, and venison—and the men drank to victory with cups full of *kumiss.* It was a powerful drink from fermented mare's milk that often made the men silly, full of bragging and laughter and jokes. Sashi drank water.

When all the food was eaten and the cups of *kumiss* emptied, the men spoke of war with Persia, and the need for unity. The need was why four brother tribes—Scythian, Budini, Geloni, and Sarmatian—gathered upon the steppes, to plan how to drive back the Persians. They wanted too much of the world. King Darius was greedy. First he would cow the steppes, then turn to conquering Greece.

Brushwood was piled high, thrust through by an iron sword. Soothsayers, using magical willow wands and linden bark to foretell the outcome, predicted victory.

Sashi stared at all the people. So many strange but familiar tribes, very much like her own. All clothed in leather and felt, aglitter with glass and gold, born to ride the steppes on swift bright-eyed horses.

Horses. Abruptly Sashi rose, bowed to her mother, her father and her brothers, then made her way slowly from the fires into the darkness beyond, as if she went to their tent with its blue-dyed gryphon.

But Sashi avoided the tent. Instead, she went to the horses.

She couldn't count them all. She knew only there were ten times ten the number of fingers on both hands, and more beyond that. They grazed contentedly under the sky, shapes and shadows in moonlight, plucking the earth bald. But come morning the tribes would move, taking tents, horses, wagons, leaving the campsite behind.

Duns, bays, browns, freed now of their gear. Tribesmen loved their horses, taking pride in their appearance, and put them in bridles plated with gold; in saddle pads made of silk and felt and wool, carefully dyed and stitched, all aclatter with beads and bosses.

What was it like, Sashi wondered, to ride free across the steppes, making thunder as you ran?

"So," someone said, "are you bored with the soothsayers, too?"

Twitching in surprise, Sashi turned quickly and stared at the intruder. The moon was full, the light good, but she didn't know the face.

The girl grinned. She glittered with gold, like the others, wearing all her wealth. Earrings, necklets, bracelets and rings. She had braided little plates into her hair, which was much redder than Sashi's brown. Her eyes were a startling blue, instead of dark like Sashi's.

The blue eyes narrowed. "Have you come to steal a horse?"

"Of course not!" Sashi glared. "Why would I steal a horse? My father has more than this."

"More?" The girl arched her brows. "Is he a king, then? *My* father is."

Sashi swallowed heavily. She had been taught not to lie, nor even to exaggerate, but the girl had caught her out. "No," Sashi said quietly. "My father isn't a king."

The girl shrugged. She was taller than Sashi, and older, with a grace born of freedom and horses. She wore a woven shirt. Her baggy crimson trousers were tucked into flat-heeled boots that rattled with bead and bone ornaments. A knife hung from her belt, and a woven bridle rode her right shoulder, looping under her arm.

She looked out at the horses, then turned back to Sashi. Her eyes were very wise as she studied the Scythian girl. "No, not stealing. Wishing you were me."

Sashi stared. "I don't even know you!"

Now the eyes were kind. "You don't have to. I saw you today, when we came riding in. Wishing you had a horse, so you could ride the sea of grass."

It hurt, because it was true. Silently, Sashi nodded, avoiding the girl's blue-eyed gaze. She saw too much with those

161

eyes. "Scythian girls don't ride horses. We ride carts and wagons, instead."

"You should be Sarmatian," the girl said briskly. "Not only do we ride, but we fight beside our men." She laughed scornfully. "Do you know what the Greeks call us?"

Sashi shook her head.

"Descendants of Amazons." She twisted her wide mouth. "The Greeks don't know everything. They only think they do."

Sashi didn't care about Greeks, not at this moment. She looked out at the herd. "Have you a horse of your own?"

"Of course. Here, I'll call him to us." The girl turned her head and whistled softly, but pitched the sound to carry. "Here he comes—see? He knows the sound of my song."

Sashi held her breath. From out of the herd came a horse, a young clean-limbed horse, dun-silver in the moonlight. His mane was clipped short. Colored tassels were braided into his tail, rippling as he moved. Ears pricking forward alertly, he trotted to the girl and set his muzzle into her hands, snuffling against her palms. He had great dark eyes heavily fringed with lashes. As the Sarmatian girl stroked his cheek, he closed his eyes in pleasure.

He was by no means a huge horse. Steppes ponies were bred for heart and quickness, not overpowering size. And he was young, not quite fully grown. Sashi thought he was beautiful. The most perfect horse she'd ever seen.

She exhaled slowly, feeling the pain of yearning swelling inside her heart. She wanted one so badly. A horse to come at her whistle, to lip softly at her hands, to snort noisily through wide nostrils and warm her flesh with his breath.

A horse she could *ride,* making thunder as she went.

The Sarmatian girl laughed as the colt brushed her face with his muzzle, then buried it in her hair. She untangled damp braids with effort, jewelry clattering, then cradled muzzle and jaw and turned him to face Sashi.

"*His* name is private," she said, "but mine is Tassya."

"Sashi," Sashi said, looking only at the dun colt.

"He's a bold bright one," Tassya told her proudly. "Fleet as wind, and gentle. Would you like to ride him with me? He's generous, he'll share."

Sashi couldn't remember the last time she had been allowed to sit on a horse. Years. Her father had put her up on his favorite mount, leading her around in ever-widening circles. The ride had been too short, but long enough for Sashi to know she could do it again. She felt it in her bones; she was a *Scythian.*

But now, at eleven, she was almost a woman, and women rode in wagons. "Oh yes," she whispered. "Oh *yes,* I would."

"Ai, so I thought." Tassya took the bridle from her shoulder and hooked the headstall over the dun's ears, then slipped the bit between his teeth. Bronze and gold ornaments flashed in moonlight, chiming as they clashed.

"I have no trousers," Sashi blurted.

"Hike up your caftan. You're wearing boots, and no one is here to see." Tassya clearly had little patience when it came to such things as maidenly modesty; to her, the horse was more important, and the magic of the ride. "Have you ridden before, and mounted?"

Sashi nodded, thinking back to her father's horse. "But I'm not very good at either."

Tassya shrugged. Turning toward the colt she sprang up, landing belly-down across the dun back. Quickly she swung a leg over and sat upright, gathering reins, then offered her left arm to Sashi. "Grasp it and swing up behind me. I've helped my sisters mount. Just don't sit back too far. Stay close to me."

Sashi caught the offered wrist and swung up, grateful for Tassya's help. She landed awkwardly, but astride, and scooted close to Tassya as the dun colt swished his tail.

"Hold on," Tassya advised, and clicked to the dun with her tongue.

At first it was a bumpy, perilous ride, for the colt didn't know Sashi. She heard the swishing of his tail, felt the arching in his spine, sensed his consternation. But Tassya spoke to him quietly, soothing him with her tone, and soon enough he settled.

Grass slapped at Sashi's boots and broke off against her shins; bits of it worked into her boots, making her ankles itch. But Sashi paid no mind. She was riding a horse. Call her *centaur*, even Amazon; Sashi didn't care. So long as she could ride.

And she was. She was *riding*. Beneath her she felt the relaxation of the colt's muscles. Felt the smooth silk of his carefully tended coat. Felt the quiet power of his muscles. And felt herself respond, remembering how to ride.

Sashi sat up straighter. Gripping the colt's sides with her legs, she became one with his motion, glorying in the ride, remembering what she was: a woman born to the back of a horse.

But the ride was much too short. Tassya stopped the colt, breaking the spell. "Enough," she said. "He needs his rest, and so do we. We go to war in the morning."

"War," Sashi said numbly, sliding off with Tassya's help. "Why do we have to fight?"

Tassya jumped down. "We don't," she said calmly. "We will harry them, instead, and drive them mad with our patience and great swiftness. Do you know nothing of the Persians?"

Sashi shook her head. "I told you—my father isn't a king."

Tassya laughed and slipped the bridle from her colt. "Persians fight differently than we do. My father tells me they use chariots, and they like to stand and fight. He says Persians *hate* people who won't face them. He says the smartest enemy will make fools of the Persians, so they'll go home in a sulk."

"Why do we fight at all, no matter how we do it?"

Tassya's smile faded. "I don't know," she said. "But King Darius wants to conquer Scythia, and we have come to help stop him."

"Will we win?" Sashi asked.

The Sarmatian girl grinned and slapped her colt on his rump, sending him back to the herd. "The soothsayers say we will. But then, they always do."

Sashi watched the colt fade away into shapes and shadows. "You're the daughter of a king. Do *you* think we'll win?"

Tassya's eyes were bright. "I think we can do anything, so long as we have our horses and a sea of grass to ride."

In the morning they went to war. Sashi found it boring, and not in the least dangerous. But then, she was in a wagon like all the other Scythian women and girls, trundling across the steppes, while the men and Sarmatian women rode off to harry the Persians and send King Darius home.

"I want to go," Sashi said, watching the clouds of dust.

Uta smiled faintly. "Our duty is to the wagons, and to seeing the men are fed."

"I'm tired of wagons and carts. I want to ride a *horse*, like the Sarmatian women do."

"They're different," Uta said quietly. "Once, we were like them, but now we rule the steppes. We're a powerful people, Sashi . . . it's a mark of honor that no Scythian woman is required to ride a horse, but to be drawn in a wagon instead. Let the men spend their days on horseback. We need no longer do it."

"Didn't you ever want a horse of your own?"

Uta's face was thoughtful. "When I was younger, before I was a wife, yes. As a little girl, of course; I think we all do. And there was a time, much later, I borrowed one of my father's fillies and spent a night by myself. It was the only chance I had."

Sashi stared at her mother. "Then you know what it's like. *You* know what it means: to ride the sea of grass."

Troubled, Uta nodded. "I know what it means."

Sashi drew in a breath. She felt as if she was being treated as an adult for the first time in her life. It gave her the courage to ask another question. "Do you wish you could again?"

Her mother stared out at the drifting dust left by galloping horses. It was all that remained of them. "Always," she said softly.

Sashi grew very tired of war after weeks of trundling across the steppes. Her father said the Scythians and Sarmatians and all the other gathered tribes were teasing the Persian army mercilessly, baiting them in one direction, then striking from another. King Darius wanted the kind of battle *he* was used to. But the horsemen knew better. The only way they could beat Persian might was to use shrewd steppes strategy.

Tassya herself echoed his words when she came riding up one night at dusk. Her ruddy braids had come loose and her face was dusty, but her blue eyes burned like the sun. "We're not fighting," she announced. "We're harrying, like gnats. Everyone says it will make the Persians lose patience, because they can't stand the waiting."

Sashi felt a pang of envy. "Do *you* harry them, too?"

"Of course." The Sarmatian girl was dressed for war. The carrying case called a *gorytus* hung at her left side. It held a Scythian bow, and arrows. "Would you like to come with me sometime?"

The question amazed Sashi for its audacity. She meant to say no. She knew she should say no. But then she thought of her mother, who had borrowed one of her father's fillies to go on a night-long ride. "You mean, go to *war?*"

Tassya shook her head. "No, no, we'll stay well back of the Persians. And anyway, we aren't fighting. We're *harrying* them, nothing more. We're driving them into a frenzy by stealing their horses, burning the land before them so they have no grazing, and picking off stragglers. Don't you know strategy?"

Sashi solemnly shook her head, hating the left-out feeling.

But Tassya's laughter was kind. "Ai, I forget not everyone has a father who is a king. I've grown up on strategy. Ai, well, they mean to tease the Persians, leading them in tens of circles until Darius gives up."

It seemed odd to think of a great king like Darius giving up out of frustration. It wasn't war as she thought of it. "Will the strategy work?"

Tassya nodded wisely. "My father says we'll harry them into madness, then send them scurrying home."

Sashi glanced over her shoulder toward the felt tent. Uta was still inside. "I would like to go," she admitted, looking at the dun colt.

Tassya nodded, grinning. "I'll come for you when I can."

Sashi waited daily for Tassya to come. But the Sarmatian girl didn't, and Sashi began to worry. Had she been killed by a Persian? Was she sick? Had she been caught in one of the fires set to burn forage the Persians needed? Or had her father found out she had befriended a Scythian girl with no ties to royalty?

And then Tassya appeared one day, glittering with gold, astride her dun-colored colt. "He had a stone bruise," she announced, "but the hoof is healed now, and he's more than ready to run."

Sashi looked over her shoulder toward the tent. She

wanted to tell her mother, but she knew what Uta would say. And so she went in secret.

Tassya took her out across the grasslands, keeping the colt in check because, she said, after so many days of rest he would be too wild for two if they let him go faster. Sashi agreed. She felt the arching of his spine, heard the slashing of his tail, sensed the impatience of his spirit. The colt wanted to run, to be free of both his riders. Only manners kept him quiet, and Tassya's experienced hands.

"There," Tassya said quietly. "See all of our people?"

Sashi stretched upward to look over the girl's shoulder. Indeed, she saw the people. Tens and twenties of people, mostly men, but with Sarmatian women as well. All gathered amidst the grass as they discussed strategy.

Tassya's indrawn breath was a hiss. "Persians," she whispered.

Sashi looked. And saw them: rank upon rank, chariot upon chariot, afloat on the sea of grass as they gathered to join proper battle.

Anger surged up, filling her voice with power. "This is Scythian land!" she cried. "This is *our* land—" But she never got to finish because her shout startled the colt. He jumped sideways awkwardly, then leaped again as a hare broke cover.

Tassya snatched at too-slack reins. *"Hold on!"* she cried.

But she was too late. The awkward, hopping jump of fear tumbled both girls from the colt's back.

Sashi landed on her side, right arm trapped. It hurt, but she knew it wasn't broken. She sat up, thinking of Tassya and the colt, spitting dirt and grass from her mouth. Thinking about how it was her fault. She shouldn't have shouted. "I'm sorry, Tassya. I'm *sorry!*"

Tassya groaned. Slowly she sat up, touching a hand to the side of her head. Blood stained her fingers. "My horse," she said dazedly, ignoring the blood on her hand.

Sashi started to answer. She wanted to apologize again, but a sound caught her attention. It was a high-pitched, shouted challenge echoed by Scythian and Sarmatian alike, tens and twenties of them, thrusting fists and bows into air. Sashi heard the word for the hunt shouted, and then all the horses were running.

Gaping, Sashi stared after the horsemen. She thought surely they would challenge the Persians now. Had she somehow started the war?

Tassya hissed in pain, fingering the bleeding bump hidden beneath braided hair. "My horse," she repeated.

Sashi stared at the Persians. She could see their lines tightening. She *had* started the war!

"We have to go back," she said abruptly, and turned to help Tassya up.

But the Sarmatian girl went white in the face and sat down hastily. "Dizzy," she mumbled, and shut her bright blue eyes.

"We can't stay here!" Sashi cried, thinking of the war.

Tassya wiped blood from her face and whistled to call the colt. The sound was thin and weak, lost beneath the noise of shouting horsemen and the thunder of their mounts.

Sashi shook her head. "I don't think he can hear you."

"Fetch him," Tassya said weakly. "You'll have to go back for a wagon—my head hurts too much to ride."

"Me! By myself?" Sashi stared at Tassya.

Tassya merely waved a hand, very much the princess. Or very much in pain.

Sashi drew in a deep breath. *Go,* she told herself. *Ride the horse, and go.*

The dun colt stood but twenty paces away, lipping half-heartedly at grass. Sashi approached so he could see her and recalled how Tassya had soothed him with her voice. Sashi sang him a song, easing her way toward him, until he lifted his head and stared directly at her.

"I need you," Sashi told him. "Just for a little while."

Big-eyed, he blinked. Sashi approached carefully, and he allowed her to touch him. He let her catch his reins and stroke his neck. His fear of the hare had passed.

His hair was soft around his nostrils, the saffron-silver of winter grass. Long-lashed eyes watched her alertly, full of unexpected trust. Sashi cupped a hand to his muzzle and felt the warmth of his exhalations.

"Horse," she said, "I need you." But the horse made no answer.

Sashi summoned all her strength, recalling how Tassya mounted, and turned toward his back. Springing up from the balls of her feet, she landed belly-down, sprawling across his back and the felt pad that served as a saddle.

The colt lifted his head up high and snorted. He moved sideways a little, shaking his head so hard all the gold ornaments clashed and rattled. Sashi bit her bottom lip and waited, draped across his back. She tried to remain calm. She felt the subtle shifting of his muscles; he wasn't used to Sashi without Tassya present too. He lashed his tail in warning.

I've done it wrong, she thought, and quickly pushed herself upright, swinging right leg across dun rump to straddle green-dyed felt. The reins were in her hands.

"We have to go," she told him quickly, before he could protest. He shook his head, swished his tail, clattered ornamentation. "Not so far," she promised. "Only to the wagons. And then others will come to help, and Tassya will be fine."

He seemed to listen. His ears flipped back toward her, then forward. He pulled at the reins a little, chewing on his bit.

"Let's go," Sashi said, and tapped his sides with her heels.

At first he didn't walk. He pranced. He *tested,* to see if she could ride him. To see if she was worthy. Sashi felt him listening to her. Saw him watching her, slewing a brown eye backward whenever he turned his head. From time to time he snorted, as if commenting on her presence.

At first the prancing scared her. And then, as she settled into his rhythm, it didn't anymore. He was only showing off. He was only saying everyone should notice how beautiful he was. So Sashi told him he was beautiful and bright-eyed and bold, but that another time for showing off might be better. Tassya needed him. Tassya needed them both.

He settled. Sashi felt it. The tension and prance faded, replaced by steadiness, and she felt the acknowledgment in him. He would do whatever she asked, because she had passed his test.

For two days Sashi was unable to see Tassya because the Sarmatian healers were tending her sore head. Uta told Sashi not to worry, that Tassya would be fine, but she still worried. It was her fault the hare had spooked the colt; how could she *not* worry? And so she did, paying little attention to her mother when Uta said something about the strategy succeeding, thanks to a lucky spur-of-the-moment hunt.

Her mother was smiling, but the words meant nothing to Sashi. She didn't think war half as important as Tassya's recovery. She worried two whole days, until Tassya herself came to find Sashi and thank her.

The Sarmatian princess led the dun colt, all ablaze with gold and glass and his green Sarmatian felt. He snorted a greeting to Sashi.

"Walk with me," Tassya said, and grinned at Sashi's surprise. "Until my bump is gone, I must walk, or ride in a wagon. They have made me a Scythian woman, at least for a day or two."

Sashi nodded, sighing. "*You* made me a Sarmatian when I had to ride the colt."

"And a heroine, to me and to our people."

Sashi shrugged. "You'd have done it for me."

Tassya laughed. "Brought help, yes—but I mean about the hare."

Sashi colored. "I'm sorry. It was my fault. If I hadn't scared the hare, he wouldn't have scared the colt."

"Have they told you nothing?" As Sashi frowned, Tassya laughed aloud. "I said you were a heroine, and you are. When you broke the hare from cover, our people decided they'd had enough of war for the moment. They preferred chasing hares to Persians, and so they declared a hunt." Tassya's blue eyes were bright. "It offended the Persians past bearing. Darius said he couldn't understand a people more willing to hunt a hare than to stand and fight his Persians, and swore he wanted no more to do with us. No honor in it, he said, and took his Persians home."

"A hare?" Sashi asked blankly.

"When Darius questioned the chase and our honor, our king told him, 'Go weep.' " She laughed again, blue eyes bright. "He left for Persia instead."

"A *hare*," Sashi repeated.

Tassya's merriment died. Abruptly she thrust the reins into Sashi's hands. "He's yours," she said fiercely.

Clutching reins, Sashi stared.

Tassya nodded. "I make him a gift to you, in honor of your service."

"Oh, *Tassya!*"

Some of the fierceness faded. Tassya's smile was warm. "Take him, Sashi. Please. My father wanted to give you gold and glass and silk, but I knew better than that. The colt is worth the service. Metal and glass is not."

Sashi's throat hurt with the wanting of the colt. "But he's *yours.*"

"I have others," Tassya said steadily. "Ai, I've loved him well, but there are other colts to tend. You have only him."

Sashi swallowed heavily. "They won't let me keep him. Women and girls don't ride."

"It never hurts to ask." Tassya smiled a little. "We're going home tomorrow, back across the Don River. Say you will keep my colt. I *want* you to have him. You deserve him, Sashi. He deserves you."

Mutely, Sashi nodded. She was glad to have the colt, but sorry to lose the friend.

"Go on," Tassya said, "take him for a ride. This time for yourself."

In silence, Sashi jumped up onto the colt, glad of Tassya's help. The dun snorted, shook his head, swished his tassled tail. Tassya held his head, whispering to him gently, then relinquished grasp and ownership. "His name is Gryphon," she said softly, and turned away from them both.

Sashi watched her go. The Sarmatian girl walked proudly, head held high, gold and glass aglitter. There was no sorrow in her posture, only pride in heritage; in the freedom of her race.

Centaur. Amazon. A woman of the steppes.

"A strong girl," Uta said, standing by the tent.

Sashi twitched in shock and felt the colt respond. Quietly she soothed him, stroking his dun-colored neck. She licked dry lips and turned her head to look at her mother. "I have a horse," she challenged, waiting for the pain that would come with her mother's refusal.

Uta's face was solemn. "Small enough reward for the girl who ended the war. Even your father says so."

Joy bloomed in Sashi's heart. "Are you saying I may *keep* him?"

"I am saying we are Scythians, born on the backs of horses." Uta smiled and waved a hand. "Horses require riding. Go and tend to yours."

Slowly, Sashi turned her horse and rode him away from the tents, away from the people, from the masses of other horses. She wanted him to herself.

"Now," Sashi whispered. "Now, Gryphon—*go.*"

First he walked, twitching ears, waiting for her signal. Then trotted as she gave it, jogging easily. And then, as Sashi grew brave, he struck an effortless canter.

She leaned down over his neck, hugging him with her legs. Gold shone on his bridle. Tassles bedecked his tail. He was a smooth-striding, bright-eyed horse. A horse of bedtime stories. A horse to harry Persians.

Or, she thought, grinning, *a horse for hunting hare.*

And Sashi hung on, laughing, as they rode the sea of grass, making thunder as they went.

ABOUT THE AUTHOR

Bruce Coville is an award-winning author of books for children, including Doubleday's *The Unicorn Treasury*. He has contributed to numerous magazines and newspapers, including *Sesame Street Parent's Newsletter* and *Cricket*. Mr. Coville also has a special interest in theater and has written three musicals for young audiences. Formerly an elementary school teacher, he now writes full-time from his home in Syracuse, New York.

ABOUT THE ARTIST

Ted Lewin, a graduate of Pratt Institute, has been illustrating children's books for more than twenty years. A longtime wildlife enthusiast, his stunning watercolors have brought animals to life in many of the more than seventy books he has illustrated. The artist lives in Brooklyn, New York, with his wife, Betsy, who is also an artist.